ALSO BY NICK MAY

Minutemen

Molecricket

MEGABELT

NICK MAY

Illustrator: Richard Loveless

ISBN10: 1 -63199-126-4
ISBN13: 978-1 -63199-126-4
Library of Congress Control Number: 2014955287

Eucatastrophe Press
P. O. Box 841
Gonzalez, FL 32560

eucatastrophepress.com

To Danilo Salvador
for making the belt a bit easier to buckle

... and for Cal

TABLE OF CONTENTS

FOREWORD

NICK MAY

A lot can happen in five years. I graduated college, lost fifty pounds, traveled the country, got fired, gained ten pounds, released a record, got married, moved out, wrote two books, got a dog, moved cities, planted a church, and now I'm sitting in my smelly armchair on a Saturday morning in October, wondering what the next five have in store. I like change. I like ritual as well (ask my mom what happens if she bakes a pie wrong on Thanksgiving), but change is what strings us on; the ever present knowledge that things simply won't last forever. It can be good or bad, depending on how you look at it. In terms of The Megabelt, I learned that a five year shelf life for relevance in many of these pages was really pushing it. Some of the irony will be lost on you Belters as we travel into a new age of weirdness. Things here have certainly changed.

I was, however, pleased to find, upon revisiting Gil and his friends, that much of the conviction within this tale still rings (and stings) true. When I say The Belt has changed,

I suppose I mean the advantage is always switching hands. The game has gone into extra innings with no apparent leader. It's still a place where everyone goes to church, and Sunday bulletins are a currency for fried chicken, but the original ending of the book has never been a more real representation of the utter surprise this place still brings on a day-to-day basis.

I wrote *Megabelt* because I read *Slaughterhouse-Five* and cringed every time Vonnegut talked about Christians. As a story with essentially no antagonist or agenda, it served as inspiration that a book didn't have to slam its reader with a message (even a subtle one). As a story with essentially no real authority on Christianity, it served as a charge to write something about a community in which I had been immersed my entire life (something greater authors encourage lesser ones to do). All I had to do was tell the truth about the people and places I grew up with, and that truth would be greater than any scarlet thread I could weave through a convoluted literary vehicle. But don't worry about all that.

A Note on Chapter 16: I still consider the true ending to be the knock on the door, but it just didn't do to release a 5th Anniversary Edition of my first book without at least getting to see what Gil had been up to. I see 16 as a light-hearted reunion; a familiar update with no real gravity to the story. I described it to my wife as the Christmas Special episode of British television tradition. It made sense to her, and I think you'll find the new ending accomplishes its job of being a subtle nod to the original. I hope you like it. If you don't, or if Gil's story no longer identifies with you, then I fear The Megabelt has been reborn in its own ashes and taken the form of some good-natured utopia in which all wrongs have been righted and there no longer exists the need for protest or revolution. After all, a lot can happen in five years.

1

EASTER SUNDAY

G il could only remember one Easter Sunday that wasn't absolutely beautiful. It was the Easter Sunday that it rained and his mom said:

"I can't remember one Easter Sunday that wasn't absolutely beautiful." It seemed to have been somewhere close to a thousand years since Gil had participated in an Easter egg hunt, or caught the overwhelming smell of vinegar and dye in the air, or rifled through a basket full of candy on the fireplace just before church. Gil would have happily participated in an Easter egg hunt had he been invited to one in his older age. He was eighteen now. He could recall boiling the eggs or blowing out the yolk and then dipping the smelly orbs into the pungent liquid. Someone would always dye a really good egg—generously colored and evenly blue on all sides—but there was always the duckling that was ugly before it ever hatched. The person responsible was always someone who got overzealous and dipped his or her egg into one-too-many colors. It was like they actually thought that if they mixed all the colors, it would undoubtedly turn out to look like a beautiful rainbow, rather than some sickly color the same shade of bile.

When Gil was younger, his Easter basket was usually purchased at Wal-Mart by his mother one-hour prior to being stuffed with weird jellybeans, Cadbury chocolate, and Peeps. Allow me to explain Peeps. Now, one might ask:

"Why does he need to explain Peeps to me? They're tiny, yellow, sugarcoated marshmallow chicks. You bite their heads off. They're brilliant." Well, hear me out... Peeps are tiny, yellow, sugarcoated marshmallow chicks. Stop kidding yourself. You've never finished a Peep in your life. You know what Filipinos put in their children's Easter baskets? Balut. Balut is a real egg with a real chick inside. They eat them like champions. Filipino kids were chomping on real tweety birds and Gil's mom was buying him Peeps. Seeing a Filipino trying to eat a Peep would be like watching the bald guy from The Travel Channel eat a turkey sandwich. Back to mom.

"Have a great day! Happy Easter!" the checkout girl said. Gil's mother observed her for a moment and reasoned in her own mind that if the checkout girl was bidding her farewell with this religious salutation of "Happy Easter" then she must be a semi-Christian and therefore must be working instead of attending church on this holy day. It was suddenly her business.

"Do you have a church?" Gil's mom asked bravely, attempting to strike up a conversation with a potentially wayward pilgrim.

"Yeah, actually I go to St. Luke's," she replied—in other words "no." St. Luke's was the imaginary Catholic church on the other side of town with a congregation of 53 million people. You know St. Luke's—there's one in just about every city in America. Perhaps the physical structure of St. Luke's does in fact exist, but it might as well be imaginary. The intellectualist majority in places like Boston laugh at individuals for even attending church as an academic—in the Bible Belt (the area between Texas, Florida, Mississippi, and Virginia) you get grilled for not having a default answer like "St. Luke's."

Gil, like a lot of twenty-something's in the South, would occasionally visit what Belters so affectionately call "the church home." This was the church that you blow out of when you're old enough, but still return to visit as a favor to your parents whenever there's free food, weddings, funerals, or other special events—in this case—a Sonrise Easter service. Yeah, you caught it. "Son-rise." That's the kind of wit they like in the belt—perfect for the church lawn marquee.

1 cross + 3 nails = 4-given

Join us for our Sonrise Easter service 6:00 A.M.

First United Methodist Church

Gil stuck close to his parents and two brothers while at First. Their parents were the kind that had been happily married for twenty-five years. No divorce. No damage. No skeletons. They were well placed staples in the church, just like ten other couples in attendance that were all responsible for inadvertently encouraging each other to stay there. His brothers were the kind that operated well together. No rebels. No fights. No alliances. The three of them, Gil being the youngest, were made (by their staple parents) to endure the good and the bad, especially concerning church. They would later adopt this obligation to "tough it out" as their own form of self-induced loyalty, when others would begin to leave.

"Looks like you brought the whole gang this mornin' Grey!" slurred the local church Everyman. He was drunk on coffee and reeked of Krispy Kreme. The Everyman's boisterous salutation was enough to alert the entire congregation that the prodigal sons had returned once again from feasting with the swine.

"Hey guys. How's school? How are the girlfriends? How's the slop?" they all asked. Generic questions always received generic answers.

"Hey. Good. Great. Delicious."

The rest is pretty believable. One can probably guess. There were tri-fold programs and Communion cups—lawn chairs and standers who wished they brought lawn chairs. Maybe there was a fond moment thrown in there when the sun would hit the retention pond right at the perfect time. After that, it was off to the car where Gil and his brothers would make a quick stop for some breakfast. The three of them would sit in the Chick-fil-a drive-thru for six and-a-half minutes before they would remember that Truett Cathy stood for two things:

1. **Chick-Fil-A never being in Nascar.**
2. **Chick-Fil-A never being open on Sunday.**

**Both of which were sore disappointments
in the South.**

During Gil's earlier life, before he and his brothers decided for themselves how best to spend their post-church hours, Sunday afternoon was reserved for napping. Later on, Gil would realize what a genius plan the nap truly was, but for the time being, he refused to be a part of the weekly ritual. He didn't understand it.

"Sunday is the day of rest—the Sabbath," Gil's mom would say. Gil's mom thought she was Jewish—she did—regardless of what she says in this exposition. A house with no lights on in the middle of the day is a cave, and by one o' clock, Gil's family members were sleeping bears. Gil believed that 40% of his mental growth was done during these hours. If the time wasn't spent thinking, it was spent stuck in the eternal cycle between

**cabinet—refrigerator—pantry—
cabinet—refrigerator—pantry.**

After finally falling asleep from boredom, Gil was immediately awakened by Grey— his dad.

"You ridin' with me or mom?" he would ask in a rush.

"Mom," Gil replied, knowing she would be late.

"Alright, see ya in a while."

Night church. The state of mind that Gil was in had him thinking that this morning was yesterday, and that a second round of church in one day didn't really make a whole lot of sense. Night church smelled like the paper mill and felt like eating leftovers. Gil knew there would never be more than one friend available at night church, but it was like playing the Florida Lottery to see who it was going to be. As sad as it was, when the lotto balls turned up foul, Gil had his escape plans pre-mapped A through C.

A. Nursery
B. Sound booth
C. Back row

One-by-one, each plan was scratched by his dad. Grey had an excellent radar for locating Gil.

It goes without saying that Sunday night was the worst part of the week for Gil, merely because school was the next day and it was the bitter stop to the weekend. Gil's school was one of those church/school hybrids that had the balls to offer Kindergarten through 12th grade—you know the one—the place with a lion for the mascot. Most Belter schools have a lion for their mascot if only to resist originality. The lion suits any Christian school. It just wouldn't make any sense for a Belter school to have their mascot be something like a Biblical people group or a peaceful animal like a dove. Perhaps the school announcements would say:

"Tonight, it's a rival of biblical proportions! The Gator Point Jews versus the Gospel Christian Lambs of God!" It might as well have been that epic.

The drive from Gil's house to where he and Grey would drop off his brother and then move on to his own school was approximately one Big Daddy Weave or one and-a-half Stevie Ray Vaughn records long. His entire high school career was spent in a single, top floor hallway about six ft. wide and a hundred ft. long. He had seven classes, four teachers, and knew the first and last names of all one hundred and fifty kids (ranging from sixth to twelfth grade) who were confined to the hallway. His entire high school could fit on one bus, and his graduating class had a staggering twelve people in it.

"How was everyone's Easter?" Gil's homeroom teacher would ask. Most would think about answering—some would actually answer.

"Good. I was in the Easter play," said Kevin Woods. This was the kid who actually attended the church portion of the school/church. The teacher replied,

"Oh, how exciting! Who did you play?"

"Peter."

Though Peter did get to cut off an ear, this was an excellent failure in the eyes of the other students. The school/church member wore it with pride, however. In most cases, greater attention was paid to the casting of the Roman soldiers, although the popularity of the role amongst male youth was kept hush-hush out of fear of being condemned—the same as with the demon parts in the hellfire plays (for the edgier churches).

7

Regardless of its many charming qualities, a good deal of Gil's preoccupations with the Bible Belt were probably birthed on Easter Sunday.

2

ICE CREAM

A large part of the Belt saw smoking in restaurants outlawed during the '90's, so the designated smoking and non-smoking areas were instead, emphasized as Baptist and non-Baptist—not literally, but they might as well have been. The famous church joke was the one told just before lunch, perhaps right as the pastor finished the benediction. He'd say,

"Now let's hurry up and get to the restaurants before the Baptists," or "No sense in rushing, the Presbyterians have been done eating for hours now." The crowd would erupt in laughter. What each denomination didn't know was that they all made the same jokes about each other. The simple fact was that the restaurant managers and workers didn't see denominations; all they saw were bad tippers and endless complaints. Don't take my word for it. Ask any of them. They've had Christian and non-Christian. They know who you are and they'll tell you exactly what you don't want to hear.

The alternative to choosing between Christian, non-Christian—Baptist, non-Baptist, was "dinner on the grounds" as some belters call it. These dinners usually took place on the 4th of July or any other random Sunday afternoon that the trustees felt like eating KFC and cold pasta salad. It was always silently debated whether these should be called "potlucks" or "covered dish dinners." Gil was always more familiar with the idea of a "covered dish"—it made a little bit more sense to him, until it was uncovered of course. Potluck was out. The contents of the pot were seldom lucky. In fact, most of the time they were decidedly unlucky. Fish fries were always better—and it was also easier to discern what a fish-fry was. Southern churches pride themselves in their ability to fry up a load of freshly caught (a.k.a. freshly bought) catfish. Fish fries were what the men of the church lived for. It was the only thing that they would actually get up in church to announce.

"Everyone, make sure not to forget that next Sunday we will be having our annual fish-fry and softball dinner on the grounds! Men, please bring your fryers. We'll need extra." Gil had a special place in his heart for the smell of catfish and the clank of an aluminum bat on a sunny Sunday afternoon. It was something that he would take for granted later.

The softball games that took place at fish fries and whatnots weren't really anything like the church league ones. Church league was at night during the summer. The smell of grape bubble gum, hotdogs, clay, year-old trash in metal barrels and Miss McKenzie's cigarette filled the air with an intoxicating aroma. Dirty kids ran here and there sucking on whole pickles while Christian men tried their best to pretend that they were good sports; however, cursing still takes place at Belter sporting events. To go back to the pickles—the church-owned and operated concession stand was where one could get his or her supply of delicious ballpark candy, drinks, and food for cash or foul balls—but the biggest sellers at any ballpark in Gil's south, for one reason or another, were pickles; huge, raw, juicy pickles. Buy a ten gallon jug of barely-wet cucumbers swimming in vinegar, take it to a Belter sporting event and you can sell every single one, wrapped in a paper towel for ten dollars to every kid in the place—except Gil. He hated the way they looked coming out of people's mouths, all sucked and mangled, like a grenade wound.

Other church-wide recreational events included the gospel sing. The gospel sing was an event that never really took place at Gil's church, but he attended them frequently. Being that Gil's church was neither the type to put on a gospel sing, nor the type to truly enjoy one, they were usually attended by First in order to pay back another church for attending something of their own, and these "event trades" were only ever shared by groups of like-denomination. If Indian River United Methodist had attended First's Christmas play, Gil would definitely be attending a gospel sing in January. He convinced himself that the ice cream social that followed would make it all worthwhile—there was always ice cream after sings.

The group of ten or so members of Gil's church would make the forty-five minute trek to Indian River and shuffle out of the fifteen-passenger church van. The Everyman usually drove himself and would arrive quite early. The marquee on the church sign was a true work of genius,

**"You can go to Heaven with the hypocrites…
or you can go to Hell with them."**

Gil was going to find the church marquee guy one day and break his legs so he could never make the trip to the top of the ladder ever again. Indian River UMC was the church that had a single row down the middle and extra rooms in the back—a modest facility in the country with neighboring churches to the left, right, and directly across the street. Some said that the community of Indian River didn't even have houses—just churches. Gil seated himself near the middle with a couple of his friends from First.

"Glad to have you. Glad to have you," a chubby man whispered to Gil with hot and heavy breath. Gil scanned the room for people his age but only found older parishioners and babies, and then suddenly he spotted them. They were backstage—preparing for the show in the same way that he and his friends would prepare to don their spears and stab Jesus. Gil looked at them harder and tried to figure out which one in their group was him, when a boy named Bryan leaned over and interrupted his thinking.

"Pass me a pencil," he demanded. Gil stretched across the 70's orange pew and grabbed a pencil and a program for the night. He handed the pencil to Bryan and then opened the program.

Welcome to the
25th Annual Indian River UMC
Gospel Sing!

We are glad to have you!

Opening Prayer: Pastor Jerry T. Bishop
Welcome: Carol Kingsley

This Evening's Singers:

Betty Thomas	How Great Thou Art
Billy Buxton	How Great Thou Art
Wilma Louis	How Great Thou Art
Marjorie Cline	How Great Thou Art
Ted & Jessie Butters	How Great Thou Art
Rosie Bettis	How Great Thou Art
Garth Garner	How Great Thou Art
Carol Kingsley	How Great Thou Art

Closing Prayer: Pastor Jerry T. Bishop

Gil immediately grabbed an extra pencil, ripped an offering envelope apart at the seams and began drawing three-dimensional cubes and crosses with Bryan. He was spaced out before the congregation joined Betty for the 2nd refrain.

3

YOUTH GROUP

This next bit is a necessary explanation of the Belter youth group—it has very little to do with Gil's personal interactions with individuals, but rather with providing an in depth look at all the elements that are fashioned together in constructing the textbook Bible Belt youth assemblage. Gil saw the youth group at its very finest phase. The church youth group was a fundamental part of his life (considering it was the only group of friends that Gil was able to cultivate while being home schooled through much of his early education). The Belter youth group was the social infrastructure of Southern-Christian culture—and in many cases non-Christian culture as well. Here follows the quintessential definition of a "good" youth group.

Youth Group | Yooth-Groop | (Circa 1990's) noun [Sing. or Pl.]
1. A collection of teens in attendance of a church who are between the ages of ten and twenty; having any or no religious or church affiliation whatsoever.
2. A small congregation of young people that take go-karting trips, eat out after church functions and attend summer camps with rockslides.
Ex: Gil put on his "A Breadcrumb and Fish" shirt and headed to youth group.

As poignant as it may seem, Gil saw youth group as an opportunity to attempt to showcase religious emotion and spiritual interest, but then have it tumble into a big pile of boredom, anxiety, and young love.

The boredom came from being one of the few com-mitted youthies during off-months; those after Christmas and before May. These off-months were birthed from a mutant combination of school, weather, and the fact that Sonic (a popular choice for post-youth group hangouts) doesn't have an indoor seating area for when it gets cold. (Some people argue that it doesn't get cold in certain places in the Belt—then those people argue that it in fact does and it's because of the humidity. Gil argued that Northerners could never truly understand the type of cold that certain Belters experienced, given that their core temperature was set somewhere close to Hot Pocket ham.) Furthermore, the anxiety aspect came from tirelessly awaiting the next event (i.e. trips, camps, concerts, or God experiences which Belters call "mountaintops").

Finally, there's young love. This is the most misunderstood, misplaced, and oddly enough—honest components added to the pile. In Gil's case, this "love" occurred most frequently in one of two places, the first being the skating rink—which happened to be one of the three holiest landmarks on planet Earth for Belter youth groups (the other two were the bowling alley and the go-kart track, which also had strangely powerful properties for making young love connections due to their infectious strobe lighting and sounds of late '90s top 40). The second place was of course camp. There was something about Gil's particular generation and their weakness for adopting short-lived romantic connections while on trips or at camp.

There are two things about intra-group, camp relationships: the first was that they always began with a young female showing empty attraction to another male, which we will respectively call "Male B." Male A (the male in question, in this case—Gil) will then customarily submit a series of carefully placed emotions in the form of looks, withdrawal, and perhaps notes. The female will then in turn abandon her empty attraction in Male B and make a powerful connection with Male A; in many cases, your typical half-hidden, overpowered, thumb-rubbing, interlocking hand-hold

The second thing about camp relations is that they always culminate in the couple having a Dawson's Creek-style, world-shattering argument caused by one of four things: Male A talking to Female B (from the other church), Male A needing more time at the lake with his guy friends, the female needing to focus on God (which was always dismissed without hesitation as an admirable cop-out), or lastly—that the empty attraction for Male B happened to be a half-full attraction. Gil didn't put it all together yet—he was in love with the girl that would, later that week, fart in the church van and get gum stuck in her hair. Gil would later question his motives—male B would later end up sleeping with the female…during an off-month.

Gil did have some genuine experiences with God while in the youth group. He would later think of them as rather half-baked and cliché, but they were experiences that shaped him nonetheless. They would be things like quiet moments in crowds of ten thousand. Speakers at enormous rallies would make addresses in stadium-whisper.

"You may be out there saying, 'Hey Steve man, what's one cigarette gonna hurt man? Hey Steve what's the problem with sleepin' with my girlfriend or boyfriend if I love 'em?' but you know what friend—now hear me…you are missin' out on the life of an X-treme Teen for Christ!" and the crowd would explode with thunderous agreement. Gil would clap and smile sheepishly, looking from side to side at his friends who leaked tears he had never seen before and would never see again.

Gil could better relate to the musical aspect of those rallies—the songs that they would play the first night, the last night, and over the speakers at every exit on the way out. They would stay ingrained in his mind for years after and play in his room during winter months when he attempted desperately to recall what sort of formula brought that feeling, but why in the world the music just wasn't as good as the stuff his older brother listened to. There was a definite difference to Gil between the rock-n-roll behemoths of the non-charismatic Christian sphere and those within it. You may be wondering why the words "non-charismatic Christian" take the place of the all too popular "secular" tongue slider—in all truth, the late '90s saw a sort of graying of the lines between secular and Christian; a line that Gil would later compare to the fusion of black and white schoolmates. Thank God for that.

Years later, Gil would look back and remember how familiar and unpolished the whole experience was, but he couldn't help but be drawn to thoughts of pillow fights, friends, and the first real possible brush with God. In senior high, the idea of God became more real; things like camp and youth retreats were less about having fun, and more about seriously stockpiling as much forgiveness and encouragement as a young heart could hold in order to desperately make it last as long as humanly possible.

4

CAMP FIRE

The camp Gil went to every year didn't even really have a fire (at least Gil never saw one). There was a fireplace in the gym that was never lit—its hearth was used as a bench for the non-square dancing type. The square dance was the prom-like social event of the week, and the deciding factor on one's camp-made self-esteem and popularity. Gil would just sweat it out all week, watching girls get asked one-by-one as he set his sights on chicks way out of his league. The dudes who acted so cool and together, who Gil thought would never be caught dead at a square dance, were the ones who ended up rolling into the gym on Wednesday night with the girls from Trinity UMC. You know the Trinity girls—pretty with a side of holy. The whole thing confused and frustrated Gil, and he knew that the institution of the square dance was pretty much everyone's final-ditch effort to squeeze in one last bit of fun before it got serious. Gil had his fun. He and his friends would sneak out into the dorms every morning, during the wee hours and hurl metal, folding chairs onto the stone floor. Oh, the silence before impact.

Friday, the last day of the camp week, was a huge festering problem that Gil and everyone else just sort of ignored as they went throughout their daily activities; swimming, singing, eating, praying, reading, listening, eating, swimming, singing, eating, showering. Girls strangled themselves with body spray—guys used Axe for deodorant, soap, cologne, hairspray, shampoo, toothpaste, anything. Kids were getting dolled up for a night of wild emotions and crying produced by sadness that camp was over, mixed with some sort of temporary spiritual awakening. It was heard through the hallways like a giant game of telephone.

"Bring some tissues."

Gil didn't cry. Not once. Not at camp. There really wasn't anything that moving to him yet. It took everything he had to hold it back, but he wasn't going to be seen weeping with the rest of the kids who regretted their lives year after year. He understood life was hard for most of them away from camp, but his reason for attending was so he might not become just another statistic.

Evening came. The youth gathered into a dimly lit room. Soft piano was already playing. Gil thought the whole thing was sort of romantic—like a candle light dinner for two hundred. He always felt afraid of something at these things. Maybe he was scared that someone would drag him to the altar—like the camp nurse had dragged him onto the square-dance floor two nights ago—that would be uncomfortable. The music part was easy. Gil could deal with the misplaced, hullabaloo of awkward female harmonies, the ad lib lines from the Trinity girls in the verses, and the fifty to sixty people that refused to keep time during the a capella parts. Oddly enough, it was the testimony part he couldn't really stand (though there was this strange desire for Gil to see what level of detail the suicide girl would go into this time). The soft-spoken youth pastor/chaplain for the week made his way forward,

"At this time, we want to open the front to any of you who would like to share anything special this week that has happened in your life. We would ask you to please keep it brief; maybe five minutes." Gil knew five minutes was a lifetime. Some of the kids would use closer to fifteen—some would use ten seconds. No one moved for a long time. The collective effort to retract mucous sounded like someone was sanding the inside of the pulpit. A boy stood. A girl stood. The boy sat. The girl walked. The boy would try again later. The girl faced the front and shifted her weight from side to side. She wore a face like someone apologizing for a crime they didn't commit.

"I didn't want to come here this week. My mom made me come here." Silence—then tears. "But now I'm glad I did, because I've made some of the best friends ever." Some of the more boyish females gathered around. They hugged. Gil and the others clapped. He didn't understand why. Silence again. The boy who stood before, now fully prepared, made his way to the front. He stood for a couple seconds, began to cry, and retreated to his seat. Silence.

One of the Trinity girls rose. Already with eyes watering, she said,

"I promised myself I wouldn't cry." Gil mouthed the sentence word for word, like you see actors do on SNL because they've heard the lines so many times that they're just waiting for queues.

"I've been into a lot of bad stuff lately...I've been hanging out with a lot of bad people who I thought were my friends...and last semester I started cutting myself again." Gil shifted in his seat and looked around. Something about the girl's confession was entirely too intimate for the setting. Gil laughed a bit in his head. Not at the girl—but at the awkward elephant that had suddenly stumbled into the room. She sat down after saying something about a divorce and weed. There was more awkward clapping—then silence. The boy attempted again.

"...My grandma died." The boy was a blubbering mess. "I was really close to her..." More and more tears came. Strike three. The boy returned to his seat for the night. That concluded testimony time.

Finally came the point within the service that Gil dreaded a bit. The music began to play again and then seats emptied towards the altar. The only campers left in their seats were Gil and five of the new kids that had no clue what was happening and were scared out of their minds. Gil hated being visually clumped in with that group— but he had no desire to be buried beneath sixteen sobbing and freshly acquired "best friends." The Good Samaritans came. They came one at a time. Gil could see them coming from a mile away. They sat quietly beside him—no contact at first...then it came.

"Don't you wanna go down there?"

"Nah, man I'm good right here for now. Thanks," Gil replied.

"Come on. Let me pray for you" he persisted. Gil loved his heart for it—but really was just fine alone. The Good Samaritan gave up soon enough. Later, he would be the guy that didn't want anything to do with God, and Gil would wonder what was more ironic; whether the kid was like that then, or whether Gil knew the kid would be like he was later. Others would come that Gil didn't mind so much. While his head was lowered, a hand would find his back and stay for an unusual amount of time. He never knew who it was.

Gil always remembered the eternal question that would surface and resurface all throughout his life, and for the sake of irony, we won't even ask it. If you live or have lived in the Bible Belt, then you already know what the post-camp question always was, is, and ever will be. If you don't know, ask someone from the South. They will tell you in as much poetic reprise as possible. Gil knew the answer...here it is all you heart-broken, fallen mountain climbers of summer camp...

Seasons.

5

Back Slider

There was a popular term amongst Gil's peers; one that had found its way into the pop-Belter vocabulary during the mid '90s—"Backslider." Other forms included: "Backslide," "Backsliding," "Backslid," "Backslidden," and to use it in a sentence:

"Gil, by the end of his senior year, will have backslidden ten times."

It was the kind of phrase that just rolled off the tongue like a slimy eel. The first time Gil heard it was at a revival. The evangelist (who is the person who delivers the revival in a tweed picnic basket from across the country) was referring to individuals who have not appeared in church for a long time.

"Friend, if you're away from the family of believers, and you're off doing your own thing—then you are backslidden and in need of repentance!" he would say with a sweating forehead and bulging eyes. If it isn't clear by now, backsliding has to do with an individual falling away from grace, which Gil later determined to be the grace of the church rather than the grace of God. The term became so familiar to Gil in later years that he began to hear it in almost every manner of sermon or dialogue.

"Jen is backslidden."

"I heard. Let's pray that her boyfriend doesn't backslide as well."

Gil just imagined a thick filet of a person's back skin sliding off of their body and revealing their feeble spine. Backslider.

There was redemption for the Backslider—he could get into the position where he could tack the name onto someone else. If one could make the first accusation—they were safe. One of Gil's close friends, Wayne (whose favorite claim to fame was being the only guy to ever be kicked out of the church by the pastor) had a way of reversing the undertones of accusations made against him. Wayne would be gone, away from church for long stints of time; dealing with family. Dealing with the law. Dealing with himself. Upon returning to the church, several of the authority figures would approach him.

"Been prayin' for you Wayne."

"Why?" Wayne would ask.

"Just haven't seen you around, that's all." Wayne's method of reversal was quite funny to Gil. In order to switch the situation and kill the question, Wayne, (from then on upon returning) would immediately approach the authority figure and catch them completely off guard.

"Been prayin' for you Pastor." The shock of irony was always enough to send the adults into a confused outrage and the kids into open laughter. Wayne was the guy who would later be seen smoking a Red with a faded tattoo running down his arm that said,

BACKSLIDER

Gil quickly built up an aversion to the term and often feared being referred to as one. That same fear was what kept so many churches in Gil's hometown so tight-knit. There was a girl named Nora from a church across town that Gil had met on several occasions while attending a church league softball game or a joint-church gospel sing and ice cream social. Nora and her friends were in the midst of a full-on mutiny. One thing had led to another and before long, she and her Waynes and Bryans were packing up and moving out (of church). Now Gil stood on both sides of the spectrum. On one hand, Nora would tell him about all the things that were misplaced about her church, and why she had to leave; while on the other hand, Gil was seeing people leave from his own church.

It always surprised Gil the most when he would see someone from his church leave and disappear for months— maybe years, and then run into them at a show or whatever. Upon the event of individuals leaving his physical sight, Gil would immediately assume the worst for the person in question. As hard as it was for his brain to resist, it had been ingrained in his mind that the person must have been in need of some fresh air. Maybe they needed to commit

some sins and get it out of their system (as if there was a system for depositing and withdrawing X number of sins). Maybe they were bored, tired, or ashamed—regardless, the slimy term always entered his mind. The most surprising fact to Gil was that the backslider was almost always in better condition than even Gil himself was. They weren't lost at all; in fact, they had never had it more together. This was like what was happening with Nora, and that was the case 90% of the time. The other 10% was reserved for the darker story.

Years after seeing an old friend slide out of the back pews, Gil would come across them while renting a movie or registering at the community college. Gil would have heard from others that so and so was pregnant and living with a guy who she used to date in high school. Being prepared for the worst, Gil would smile and approach So and So.

"What's up! How are you?" Side hug. Don't crush the baby.

"I'm good. I'm pregnant," looking down.

"I heard! What's your boyfriend's name again? I don't think I've met him."

"William. He works at the paper mill," looking up again.

"Cool, cool."

"Yeah, he's cool. He can't wait to be a daddy. How's you're dad?"

"He's good. Mom's good. Still doing the Jewish thing." Gil's mom thought she was Jewish—she did—regardless of what she says in this exposition, "Haven't seen you around…"

"I know. I've really been meaning to come by the church and see everyone. I just don't know what they would all think. I don't want them all saying, 'hey, look at the backslider.'" This was the most sobering moment for Gil. Just when he would think he had figured it all out, a bomb would drop on him. If he could swear that the McKenzie brothers were out running a drug ring, he would find that they were dual worship leaders at a church Gil had been thinking about visiting. If he could swear that So and So was living a wild life without regret, she would actually be scared out of her mind that her friends would pick her apart for getting knocked up. Gil suddenly wanted nothing more than to be assumed—with the rest—a backslider.

6

RED LINE

The overwhelming trend among Belters in their twenty-something's (and even younger) was to escape the fate of So and So by getting married as fast as earthly possible. Gil was eighteen and he had friends who were married that couldn't legally buy alcohol. There was a couple like this that had graduated with Gil from his small private school. This couple had been the symbol of purity and patience in the midst of a tainted world. They were the beacons of hope for all young couples courting their way through adolescence with the permission of their parents. Their names were John and Kristy, and there were thousands of them in the Belt. Gil and his friends silently envied John and Kristy.

The apartment.
The maturity.
The sex.

Kristy's younger sister had married even earlier than she had. Forget alcohol, Gil had friends whose younger siblings were having sex before they could legally watch it in a movie.

Gil was backsliding one night with some of his school friends in a parking lot (gossiping, staying out past curfew) when the subject of John and Kristy suddenly came up. Someone said they wanted to have a relationship like the two of them and all of a sudden, puke in the form of vowels and consonants joined in sequence began spewing.

"You know John and Kristy have done stuff, right?"

"Like what?" Gil replied with an almost angry look—the kind of look you give someone when they mess up your way of thinking.

"Like stuff, dude," another replied. Gil was apparently the only one who still retained that embarrassing lack of knowledge that comes off as innocence.

"They have sex or something?" Gil asked.

"Well I don't know if they've had sex, but John did tell Bryan that they got scared she was pregnant one time." Confusion swept through the empty parking lot. Gil reacted.

"Dude, how can you think you're pregnant without actually having sex?"

"I don't know. Maybe they did."

"No they either did, or they didn't—there is no maybe…" Gil laughed.

This pregnancy scare that Gil's friends were referring to is the same kind that promiscuous young Belter couples get when they lay in a bed and kiss for an hour and then the girl is a day late having her period that month. There is a common misconception (pun kind of intended) that kissing, frontal hugging, looking at, laying by, or sharing a blanket with a girl will in fact, get her pregnant—especially if she is a Christian. As convincing as it all may seem—pregnancy (as we all know) only occurs when there is hand-to-boob contact.

Gil had always heard of the fine red line that lies between one's conscience and sexual act. This line was one that could only be defined, at first, by one's parents, but then would later be defined by one's self. The theory of the red line is all well and good beyond the simple flaw that it is never specifically defined. Most Belter parents position the red line for their dating teens somewhere between talking and closed mouth kissing—though the kissing is rather out of sight, out of mind. The line is of course, not immovable. It shifts without ceasing. It was something that Gil learned quickly—if you define the red line, you'll cross it over and over—and it only slides farther and farther away. The key was that there was no key. Setting boundaries was more like setting goals. Gil found that defining the red line was like speaking a self-fulfilling prophecy, and crossing it was a disappointment of mega proportions.

Gil's final years in the youth group included several retreats focused around abstinence and the red line. You know these retreats—the ones that put young people's minds more on sex than off of it. Gil would hear about really cool "true love waits" retreats that the rockslide group and Trinity would go on. Maybe they would feature a Christian comedian or a great youth band—maybe they would even give out genuine, sterling silver "true love waits" rings (the ones with the power to save your virginity). Gil would occasionally come across females wearing these, claiming to be married to God...Gil always found it funny and strange. The retreat that Gil's group went on was more of a homegrown event. The same woman from church who (in normal conversation) always spoke so viciously about the idea of sex and how disgusting it was, often was the one speaking about how beautiful it was between a married couple.

"On your wedding night, it will be a beautiful thing of God; to share what you've been saving your whole life—the entire awkward, ill-prepared, ill-informed, painful, bloody mess of it all." So she never said that last part, but she might as well have been implying it.

From what Gil later understood, marital sex between two virgins had no resemblance to the kind of sex you see movie stars having in white satin sheets with a backdrop of floor to ceiling windows displaying a New York nights-cape. Gil heard that it was quite an opposite let down. The porn-esque expertise that every man and woman was supposed to posses was often replaced with solid darkness, timidity, and novice brides seeking refuge in hotel bath-rooms. It sounded more like a middle-school physical than a honeymoon. Gil attended quite a few weddings of Johns and Kristys. They were all relatively uniform in nature. The bride wore a dress the same white as fresh parking lot paint (as to accentuate her virginity). Guests would say,

"Oh, how beautiful! Those earrings really bring out your virginity!"

"Kristy, that veil is amazing! It goes wonderful with your shoes and virginity!" They'd have a ceremony riddled with religion and dance their first dance to "I Can Only Imagine."

Who truly knew how many times John and Kristy's red line had been reset. Their secret was as safe as Coca-Cola, and the church bells rang in exultation of the union of perfect purity and love. Gil, Nora, Wayne and the rest of their fledgling bodies, still ages from a time when their life and love would be validated, stood and watched as streams of bleach-white light beamed from the windows of the blue Toyota Camry—a recent wedding gift from Kristy's father in applause for his prized daughter's wonderful behavior and skill.

One year would pass. Gil would grow tired of hatching eggs in his stagnant life, and begin wondering if there was more out there for a twenty-something with nothing to offer. Nora would finally show some affection towards male A, and Wayne would spend his first and last paycheck from wherever to get the tattoo that would claim his soul in the name of the Belt. John and Kristy would erase the red line altogether and replace it with a black one beneath their signatures stating "irreconcilable differences." That was the closest option to, "we got married too early because it was too hard not to have sex, and we didn't want to deal with the agony of being human, getting pregnant out of wedlock and suffering the unending torment of our parents, family, church and God." Meanwhile, So and So would have her baby and celebrate her third year with William. They would get a pizza, rent a movie, and sit with their son between them on the couch in their apartment. So and So would write a note to herself on a pizza napkin,

find a church

7

MEGA CHURCH

Gil had heard mystical, fabled tales of churches in far away places, whose worship and teaching was actually relevant to a modern culture.

"Must be some kind a' demon church!" old man Malcolm would say on the steps of the grocery store—as he glared at the billboard of a smiling couple, inviting onlookers to "Compass Point" –a mega church on the edge of town. Gil would agree in sarcasm.

"Yeah, what kind of church has happy people in it?"

"Beats me kid…" Malcolm replied.

A "mega church" by definition, is a church with two thousand or more members in attendance each week—but typically, mega churches become noted as mega churches at around ten thousand attendees. Compass Point was in the two thousand bracket. For now, Gil would ignore the invitation from the happy couple on the billboard, piggy-backing their way down the beach.

Gil was swamped with other questions. Why had all the rockslide youth groups disappeared? What happened to Trinity UMC? Gil had finally sprouted wings, and had nowhere to fly at all. He would visit the churches that were booming five years ago, and the life would have been sucked out like rattler poison. Gil and his older brothers were astonished at the idea that the youth group was no longer on top, and that church was no longer popular.

"How about Seawind Chapel?" Gil would ask.

"Tried that before. So what—they have train graffiti on the wall. Big deal," his oldest brother replied.

"What about Prosperity Fellowship?" Gil's other brother would ask.

"The one that looks like a gold-acrylic heaven inside? Don't think so, bro," Gil replied. It was then that Gil remembered that Nora had told him about a church she had been visiting for the last few weeks on the edge of town.

"What about that Compass place?" Within thirty minutes, the three brothers were following signs pointing the way to something called a "worship center" and had been greeted by sixteen greeters already.

"Welcome to Compass."

"Welcome to Compass."

"Welcome to Compass."

Gil entered the packed auditorium and immediately wondered where in the world these couple thousand people had been hiding for the last decade. Surely Walmart and the mall were empty. They were seated in the very back just as the opening songs had ended. The lights went out and a screen at the front lit up with graphics accompanied by an Arcade Fire song with booming volume. Where in the world was he? In the last five years, Gil hadn't come across one person who had heard of the band, and this church was playing one of their songs over a big, bassy sound system at a point in the service where he was used to hearing the Methodist Doxology.

One solitary head turned and looked at him. It was Nora. She mouthed,

"What are you doing here?"

"I don't know," Gil mouthed back. Nora smiled and turned back around. Gil wondered when the man on the stage was going to leave and let the actual pastor come up. He was doing some monologue, pretending to be some guy just talking about God, sparrows, and something about not worrying. He did this for a good twenty minutes and then, to his utter surprise, Joel and Dennis McKenzie took his place on stage and began leading worship songs with the rest of the band. Gil suddenly realized, in his distraction, he had mistaken the pastor for a regular guy and missed the actual message. He was in a very foreign situation.

Compass was the kind of place that played all rock-n-roll sets on Sunday morning and often had a special song by a "non-charismatic Christian" band to accompany the message, which was projected on ten screens across the worship center. The "worship center" was an enormous venue otherwise known as a "sanctuary" but it was never referred to as a "sanctuary" because that sounded too archaic. By this point in time, it's safe to say that the reader is familiar with Compass—or places likes it. It's modeled after bigger churches with bigger faces and bigger facilities. Guys with cones flag you into your parking area like flight control, and you are bombarded with handshakes, back pats, and so much literature you basically need a binder to carry it all. Walking into the place feels like walking into a museum or a modern art gallery. Parents register their kids with a computerized cataloger and receive some sort of technology to be notified if their children have any complications while inside the nursery area not quite unlike Chuck-E-Cheese.

The elementary-age kids spend their Sunday mornings watching a fully plotted, fully planned, extended skit accompanied by songs, dances, and other visual stimulation reminiscent to Imagination Movers or Rugrats On Ice. The youth age kids (which are more or less a collection, rather than a group) pass their Sunday mornings in a setting almost the same as the adults, with rumpus music and a message from the "Student Leader." The post-youth service foosball and ping-pong are out the door and replaced with Guitar Hero and Halo III kiosks. The main services (choose one of the ten that occur between 8:00 A.M. and 9:00 P.M.) feature a random band and speaker rotation accompanied by lights, lasers, and smoke. It took Gil a while to get used to the rave-like atmosphere but he learned to prefer the smoke phazers and robo-scans to the old party strobe and fog machine that smelled like piss in the youth room at First.

Gil, his brothers, and Nora were eating lunch later, fantasizing about church—an odd feeling for Gil.

"Did we miss Sunday school?" Gil asked.

"No. They don't have it. They have small groups instead," Nora answered.

"Small groups?" Gil's brother inquired.

"Yeah. You go to someone's house and read and pray and that kind of thing," Nora replied, acting as if she didn't ask the same exact question three weeks ago.

Compass Point would be the church that would win Gil and his brothers over, but they soon came to understand that there were many things about the mega church that they were not accustomed to, for example: Gil's idea of a youth camp was a week-long retreat staying in a dirty cabin in the woods—Compass's youth camp was a bit different. If there weren't major worship bands, famous speakers and lush hotel rooms—it wasn't camp. The worship team (which Gil joined on account of hearing that the only way to feel like something more than a visitor was to get involved) actually adopted a professional attitude and practiced with purpose. Finally, Gil took into account that there were seven words used frequently in the mega church vocabulary:

**Relevant. Environment. Ministry. Element.
Resource. Tool. Art.**

Gil didn't know what any of it meant, but he was determined to find out what the Monologue Man was saying.

8

FATHER'S DAY

Father's Day often felt so much more difficult than Mother's Day. Mother's Day was easy. Here were the instructions:.

1. Get mom a card.
2. Tell mom I love her.
3. Eat lunch with family.

When Gil was very little he could remember participating in those specially orchestrated things for moms in the church on Mother's Day. The pastor would say,
"Mom's, if you'll look down the aisle you'll see your child coming towards you with a special gift." It was usu-

ally a rose or some sort of pendant from a Christian store called The Upper Room or something like that. Regardless of how lame the whole thing seemed to Gil now, it made so much sense to his mother, and the mothers of everyone else. He never understood why the day for dads and the day for moms were so closely related.

Gil felt like Father's day should be called Generational Recognition Day—a day to recognize the legacy of men with offspring. Let's face it—you get a man a flashlight or a wrench with a Bible verse on it, you are throwing your money away. Sure, what man wouldn't love a new grill or chrome toolbox, (which is what women immediately think of anyway) but all a father really wants is to hear:

"Dad, I ran out of gas down the road. Can you bring me a can?" He may complain—he may not—the point is, Gil's dad would feel like a dad when his son had no clue how to read a W-2 or change a tire. Basically, it was Gil's job on Father's Day to do nothing more than make a mental note of the fact that his dad knew more than he did. This was easy enough for Gil.

**1. Tell dad happy Father's Day
(more-so as a favor to mom)
2. Do what dad asks all day long.
3. Save the card money and use it on gas instead.**

The hard parts came for other people Gil knew—to some of them it looked more like:

**1. Stay home.
2. Call mom.**

3. Get drunk.
4. Call dad.
5. Cuss him out.
6. Sleep it off.

Wayne's dad had died when Wayne was only three years old. First he names his generation-Y baby Wayne, and then he goes off and dies…not racking up good father points so far. Wayne's mother had waited about eight years to remarry. By the time Wayne was eleven, he had built up enough mojo to attempt to withstand demands from his step dad. In so many words, Wayne raised himself. Father's Day was number 10,000 on his list of priorities that was five items long. The last thing he had was a father—the last thing he ever wanted to be was one. The latest Gil had heard, Wayne was gone; living in Chicago with a friend, cultivating a life fertilized by factors too numerous to mention.

The Everyman was a father of two. His sons were stocky hunter types, maybe Gil's age. They were the kind of guys you only saw on Easter and Father's Day. For all Gil knew, they were just like him. He had learned not to speculate. The Everyman was proud because he had defeated his own father in a self-made competition to do better. His own past paternal relationship was one for the books. Once every six months to a year, (during the Everyman's early childhood) a man with a wiry beard would return home from sea with unwanted gifts forcefully given to him, his mother, and younger brother. That was back when the Everyman was the Everyboy—the one who cried in bed, listening to the man with the wiry beard sing angry songs in the ring with his mother—round after round.

Nora would buy her father something incredibly practical, but it would be added to the vault as homage to the fact that seasoned fathers become detached from desires for material things overtime. Gil thought that one day, some entrepreneur would come along with the idea to take these dead gifts (you know the ones—tools, electronics, neck ties, thoughtful investments) and hand them over to new fathers with children too young to buy them good gifts while they really want and need them.

So and So would post something ambiguous on an internet social network that basically implied that she would never forgive her father for leaving her when she was a baby. Gil always reasoned that it was more difficult to hate a mother than a father, and hate God in turn because according to Christian belief, he is one—but it was hard to say for sure.

Gil made it his errand to locate the most obnoxious church sign imaginable for Father's Day. He was a special fan of the ones that spoke for God.

> **"You know what I want for Father's Day?**
> **You in church.**
>
> —God"

There was one of three things happening in these signs: either someone had found a very contemporary translation of never before seen texts in scripture, God was secretly writing notes on church marquees around town, or pastors were making defamatory claims and forging God's signature. Gil would have discovered the sign while driving from church to meet his parents for Father's Day lunch at some restaurant that serves food close enough to southern style. This was a rare occasion for Gil on Father's Day due to the fact that Grey rather appreciated a home-cooked meal on his special day over treating himself to a costly lunch. They would sit non-Baptist of course, and be served sweet tea by an older Korean waitress who seemed to have been raised by people from Indian River.

"How-tee yaw!" she would say with a confusing accent.

That was usually the extent of Father's Day for Gil. One can probably by now begin to understand how certain holidays (especially those created by Hallmark) become so repetitive in the Belt. Gil had sometimes thought seriously about never celebrating these things ever again, but then took into consideration the type of flack he would get for it. Was it okay to celebrate something over and over just because a culture taught you to? It reminded Gil of a time recently when he decided, on a whim, to not place his hand over his heart during the Pledge of Allegiance at a friends high school graduation. He received all kinds of nasty looks. Some of his friends said it was disrespectful. It wasn't that Gil didn't respect his country, or what the flag stood for; in fact, he'd probably put his hand back some-day—he had just been made to repeat a ritual again and again every morning of his high school life, and the first event featuring a pledge to the flag since then, happened to be at that moment, and he felt that he had every right not to participate. Go ahead. Get it out.

"That's anti-patriotic!" one reader exclaims. "Bla bla bla bla bla!" says a book-blogger whose opinion really matters.

Gil had no complaints about his own father, but he knew plenty of people who had complaints about theirs. It was like all the schools in the Belt that received extra funding for high scores on standardized tests (one of America's most catastrophic conventions) versus all the schools that were cut for having scores that were way too low. Gil was having a hard time celebrating Father's Day solely because his father was a good father. Maybe it should have been called "Good Father's Day."

If one was to embrace the all-too familiar belief in the parallel between an earthly father and a heavenly father—then Gil's mental God was a church-going man with an ape's hands and a love for baseball. Nora's was a man who spoke the language of the people, liked coffee, and had a powerful mustache and firm stance. So and So's mental projection of God was a man who had accidentally made her and moved on to better materials. Old man Malcolm on the grocery steps pictured his dad as the man on the Quaker can. Kristy saw a man with lots of money and no time, John—an empty seat at graduation. Wayne saw God as a guy he barely knew who kept trying to tell him how to live, and The Everyman saw his God as a silhouette in the doorway, and an awfully long night.

9

Sweet Tea

Gil had a strange fascination with the concept of time and how the present is only present now. He believed that humans had this idea in the back of their heads that if one comes through something, (a difficult time, a good time) then it is over—never to be endured or enjoyed again. Gil hated being sick to his stomach, and the idea of throwing up scared him to death, but even in times when he was completely healthy, Gil knew there would come a day when he would again have to talk to the toilet water. When Gil was seven years old, playing Power Rangers with his friend Cal, they were the realest moments of his entire life—but today he could barely remember them. Cal was a memory of Gil's that was slowly leaving him as age came on. Perhaps it was easier for Gil to recall memories with friends he still held in close contact with, rather than the ones with those who had long since been gone.

Gil, a year after performing a quadruple by-pass church transplant, found himself sitting in a corner of an ancient wooden chapel, back at the same camp he had attended his whole life with First. He was with the same kids, though they all had different faces. Cal had sat there next to him; in the realest moment either of them had ever seen. It was there that the two of them decided to follow the then-extremely popular trend of CD crushing. Gil's oldest brother had just recently joined the movement and destroyed every piece of music he owned that didn't mention God or Jesus, and in an attempt to justify it, made Grey incinerate thousands of dollars in vinyl. It made sense to Cal and Gil to go and shatter Cal's rap collection on the steps of the chapel. It all seemed glorious then, but years later; those records would find a way back into their collections. That would be when Gil would compare the graying of the lines between secular and Christian to the fusion of black and white schoolmates. It was something that had to happen, and Gil was glad it did. Now, that moment with the CDs was as hazy as the other side of the candle lit room. Gil was trying desperately to rendezvous with God-like secret agents do with their contacts in midnight cafés or mammoth libraries…but God was not there.

"This is right where I left him!" reasoned Gil in his head. Gil retraced his steps to a moment when Cal had recently died and Gil was sitting in that corner at another time. A group of young campers felt they had failed to reach God in hopes of fixing their friend, and Gil had finally found something refreshing to cry about. God was there, then.

Cal had walked with them at an earlier time, and suddenly Gil was there. The corner was filled with a pile of kids praying for God to see it fit to do something they had never seen before. Cal was in the middle—alive. Gil left that memory and went further back. He was sitting with Cal in a kitchen when they were fourteen. Cal was holding his new cell phone over a large glass of sweet tea, when he absent-mindedly dropped the shiny device into the nectary drink. Both of them laughed hysterically. The phone was ruined—he finished the tea. Gil leaped back to the present moment. He sat wondering why he couldn't orchestrate a spiritual experience to mimic previous ones. Why were there no refreshing tears? If there was one thing that the Bible Belt had taught him, it was this:

If all else fails—mountaintop experience WILL occur at camp.

Gil was lost. Where would he be if he couldn't even get his one dose of God that year? He was drawn back to a time when a senior camper was explaining that people do God an injustice when they compartmentalize his ability to move in lives to a camp experience or something like it.

"I want to start at a higher place from the beginning. Instead of letting mountaintops be the resuscitation of faith—allow them to be sustaining moments," he told them.

It could have very well been one of the most profound pieces of insight that Gil and Cal had ever received. The senior camper was like a wise sage, though he was probably younger than Gil was presently. That moment with the senior camper was so clear to Gil when he was twelve or thirteen. It made so much sense to him then, but Gil seemed to have forgotten everything now. In a way, it was sort of superstitious; how Gil would attempt to clone experiences with God. It began to make him feel quite selfish for only caring about what was in it for him, when he was supposed to be ensuring that new, fledgling campers received the same experience that he once did. Someone did it for him, after all.

Gil later began to embrace the act of doing things behind the scenes. It was Compass Point's creed to provide service and hospitality to all of their guests (regardless of how ridiculous the extent seemed to be). You've heard the term seeker-friendly. Some Belters disagree with the motives of a seeker-friendly church. They believe that perhaps church should be a gauntlet of sorts—testing one's will and ability to adapt to the surroundings already in play, rather than showering them with versatile facilities, applicable teaching, and WiFi. Some of the volunteers at Compass had made it their prerogative to leave the church when their services would go unnoticed or un-thanked for long periods of time. Gil wondered what position Jesus would take at Compass. Would he be one of the eighty-nine greeters outside? Would he direct traffic? Perhaps he would serve Starbucks coffee and Krispy Kreme donuts (that's right—as indie as Compass was, they still served the Everyman's favorite pre-service hors d'oeuvres).

Gil finally understood that if he wanted to spend his life doing something more than whining about mountaintops gone amiss, he was going to have to freely give of himself expecting nothing in return. If he was to stay on the course that he was headed in, it would eventually take the death of another friend in order to place him back into his special corner with God. The loss of Cal being the catalyst for Gil's closeness with God was like the need for global catastrophes to happen in order to unite certain parts of the world. People sit and wait passively for planes to crash into buildings so resolve will flood the Mississippi and break the levies and rush over Thailand in the form of tidal waves past super models hanging for dear life onto coconut trees. Couples break up and get back together and break up and get back together so they can feel some weak reanimation of a love long lost. Gil lived in a sick world.

Gil could remember asking his parents, on several occasions, why John F. Kennedy was such a good president. "He was a man of the people," they would say. "He was so young and the whole assassination thing was just tragic." Gil was born too late to draw an opinion for himself, but everyone he asked said something similar.

**JFK was a great president because he was young
and he was killed.
Check.**

Gil's history teacher at the school/church hybrid (who was solely responsible for Gil retaining any information whatsoever after graduating) used to talk about the young president.

"JFK asked Americans to sacrifice themselves in order to obtain a greater good." Gil thought it was an interesting idea, but was sure that he had heard it before, in one form or another, from the mouth of some Nazarene man.

Gil sat in a chair on the front deck of his house one afternoon beneath the shade of a pine tree, drinking a glass of sweet tea. He laid his head back and was surprised to see a sparrow sitting high above him in the tree. His thoughts were immediately drawn to what the Monologue Man had said about the sparrow and worry. Gil was reflecting, drawing lines in the condensation on his glass when a missile of white matter splashed into his drink. Gil stared at the sparrow's gift as it acclimated itself into the cold, sugary contents. His thoughts were on Cal, and on laughing about the cell phone. Gil spat on the deck and changed chairs. He finished the tea.

10

GOD GOD

Once upon a time, Gil had conventions. There was a method to the Bible Belt madness. Believe it or not, there was a time when it made sense to Gil to participate in all the little things that were ingrained into his head at a very young age. He never questioned whether it was wrong to drink—wrong to smoke. Gil would sit down at the table for dinner with a hot plate of food in front of him and he knew what came next. Gil's mom would have lit the menorah candles and would say a traditional Hebrew blessing.

"I know we're not Jewish, but I just thought this would be nice," she would say. Gil's mom thought she was Jewish. She did—regardless of what she says in this exposition. When people around you do something for so long, you begin to do it too and it all starts to make sense. Without order and convention, the Belt would have been a very nasty place to grow up.

Gil, a year into attending the mega-church, had begun to lose some of those hardwired traditions and understandings that had been fused to his core theological skeleton. Gil began to call this the "Big G syndrome." The "Big G syndrome" is the weirdness people get when they spend an entire Instant Messenger session typing in lower case, and then suddenly when the word "God" comes up, it's written with a capital letter. This was a default reaction. Gil thought back to a time when he was very young. He was taught in school that the name of God is capitalized, unless it's a pagan god. The name of the devil is lower case, because he isn't shown the same props as the Big G. Gil wondered why the little gods in competition with the Belter God still got to be called gods, so long as they were written in lower case. Gil always imagined a meeting between God and the gods. Big G would say,

"Alright, settle down. Here's the deal: we're all gods here right? We'll acknowledge this, but Buddha, Allah, Krishna, Vishnu, all of you—you're all god, god, god, god and god—I'm God. We square? Alright, I'll notify the World Grammar Society." There were tons of little things along those lines that Gil had attempted to reprogram in his mind. This was not to say that the God of the Belters shouldn't be respected with a capital letter, but the question as to why Belters do things the way they do, was asked.

Nora and Gil were driving together one day when Nora suddenly and violently sneezed onto the steering wheel of her car as she pulled to a stop at a red light.

"Bless you," Gil said without thinking.

"Thank you," Norah replied. Gil immediately replayed the situation in his head. It was like slow motion.

Gil had heard before that saying, "bless you" came from people long ago believing that when a person sneezed, demons were exiting their body. Gil didn't believe that demons were exiting Nora via her nostrils, but his reaction came like clockwork. He could see it now. There were lots of small imps and minions of the devil, kicking back in Nora's body. Suddenly, a phone rings somewhere and a demon in Nora's lungs picks up:

"Yes? You're sure? Wow that was fast. Alright we'll be right out." The demon hangs up the phone and heads up stairs where the rest of his friends are watching Bewitched, or Harry Potter, or Snow White, or whatever Belters deem satanic entertainment down in the South. He'd say,

"Yo! Listen up! I just got a call from little d himself! We're getting flushed out of here in ten to fifteen!" Nora's nose begins to tickle. Some of the smaller demons turn abruptly from a game of D&D. The party is over. Hundreds spring to their feet and begin scurrying about in panic, gathering their belongings: pokers, prodders, tridents, matches, pentagrams—whatever they can grab. Suddenly, they are all sucked out of the room with the most powerful force imaginable and hurled through Nora's mouth and nose. One of the demons would yell,

"I hope she's alone!"

Gil is there to foil their plan.

"Bless you," he says, as the demons disintegrate in mid-air.

"Noooooo!" they cry, as Gil's blessing banishes the demons for eternity.

It seemed to Gil like most of the rituals that Belters (and in many cases, non-Belters) participated in, were for the most part, types of homemade blessings. Christians in the South had come to believe that there was some sort of power living within certain combinations of words and obsessive-compulsive acts. Perhaps what affected Gil the most was that he spent most of his life believing that the rest of the world thought very much in the same way he did. Regardless, by the time Gil set his hands upon the doors of Compass Point, he had developed a very distinctive set of amendments to old rules.

Gil had made quite a few changes since he graduated from the church/school hybrid, which included: changing churches, changing friends, dating Nora, and he had just gotten an acceptance letter from the junior college! Gil was ecstatic. The acceptance letter was the kind they have pre-made and already stuffed in envelopes, ready to be mailed to the address on the online application so long as either the GED or High School Diploma box is checked. It looked something like this:

Dear Future Student,

Thank you so much for considering Emerald Breeze Junior College for your higher educational pursuits. YOU'RE IN!

– Dick Flemmington, A.A., B.A.

Life was going to be different for Gil. He could smell the collegiate atmosphere already. When Gil arrived at EBJC on the first day, it was nothing like he expected. There was maybe one guy wearing a sweater-vest, everyone else was in normal clothes. There were more people his parent's age than his age. He could have sworn that he saw the Everyman drinking coffee in the student union. Finally, Gil observed a large white banner, stretched between two trees that read:

Welcome to 13th Grade!

Lunchtime came and Gil found himself sitting with all his friends from the church/school hybrid. They had merely shifted space. It was like all the parts of Saved by the Bell: The College Years that you never wanted to be a part of. Gil looked from side to side and took inventory of the world around him. There were home-schoolers still in their tweens, taking dual-enroll classes. There were male basketball and baseball players so tall they reminded him of the Alton Giant, Robert Wadlow. There were female basketball, softball, and volleyball players who didn't have a heterosexual bone in their bodies, and there were BCM kids (Baptist Collegiate Ministries) having Bible study and giving out free Chick-Fil-A chicken biscuits. Gil never went to BCM, but he always politely took a biscuit.

11

TEXT BOOK

Gil did the typical two-year degree in three years thing and was out of Emerald Breeze Junior College before any of his friends. He and Nora were still together—trying to figure out how they were going to manage a semi long-distance relationship, as Gil would attend a close-by university and return home for long weekends. He thought he had managed to proudly shape his modern apologetic mindset of "new church theology" whilst maintaining a firm grip of his roots. He was ready to face what he thought was something he had finally mastered.

Gil would be starting at the new university during the spring term and living in a dorm with some dudes—who cares—it's not important. He didn't join a fraternity. He didn't join any clubs. He tried his best not to make friends, and he handled class registration, textbook purchases, and paying fees all online. Gil declared a psychology major. He figured that given the Belt's overwhelming amount of high school graduates that planned on being elementary school teachers, he should go ahead and pick something that makes even less sense. Gil was trying to be the guy that would take a risk, make it big later in life, and be looked upon as a maverick for ever considering a liberal arts major during a recession.

Gil was a bit nervous his first day, but he never really considered the type of individuals he would encounter at a state college nestled amongst the pine trees in the heart of the deep South. It wasn't until the opening five minutes of his first psych survey course that he realized he had found quite a large liberal nugget in a place he had never dreamt of discovering one. Gil was prepared to come across some form of a Dr. Darmin, (a professor of religion at EBJC with an iron fist as the only Ph.D in the department) but he never thought there were actually professors more in-timidating than he was, until he met the five people who would tear his world a new one over the course of the next few months. For the sake of saving introductions, we'll just go ahead and pretend they're all the same person (to Gil they might as well have been). Let's call him Dr. Q.

Dr. Q was the guy who spoke daintily—but had a deep voice, wore a wedding ring—but on his right hand, and liked football, but also sewing. Beyond the questions, he was the smartest person Gil had ever met. He addressed Gil on his first day,

"What are your thoughts Mr.—?"

"Gil," Gil interjected.

"Mr. Gil," Q smiled as the class laughed lightly "—on the differences between qualitative and quantitative adolescent cognitive development?" Gil said something real stupid and almost threw up. After that, he tried very hard to mimic professor talk and copy the manner in which the more seasoned students often responded. He learned quickly that there was a language one had to speak in order to get by in this new world, and he worked very hard to adopt it. Basically—talk about politics, religion, sex, or gay sex and you're in the clear.

As the next few months of the semester unraveled, Gil began to mutate into an academic. He bought books he would never read, used words he had never used, went thrifting, smoked a pipe, and tried his hand at growing a molestache. He even tried getting to the point where he could drink straight espresso. Gil wanted to be just like Dr. Q and every other zombie in the place. Some zombies wanted brains—some just wanted to show everyone their own.

Gil wasn't sure what kind of zombie he was.

Gil soon discovered that most people at the university disliked the idea of God. Beyond that, he also discovered that what the academics truly disliked was religion. This presented a complication for Gil. He wanted to find a happy medium between staunch intellectualism and balanced Christian belief—which was about as rare as a holographic Charizard. Gil figured he had an edge against his professor types who cringed at the first sight of someone like Gil; given that perhaps he had learned how to curb some of that Belter edge. Whether he tried to display it or not, Gil trailed the green funk of the Belt behind him wherever he went. People like Q had heard every approach in the book.

Somehow, a conversation in class one day leapt into a full-blown critique of the Christian God (like many conversations did) and Dr. Q made a statement that was stunning to Gil.

"All the approaches have been taken. The new thing with churches drawing attendees is this whole 'love' thing. If you think this hasn't been done before, then you are sadly mistaken. One day, hellfire and brimstone will be a popular approach again."

Gil had been found out. Compass Point was all about inundating visitors with the love trap. It was true. Love was a very effective approach today.

Gil was confused out of his mind. He used to think that Wayne was the most unreachable person alive. Wayne seemed like a cakewalk compared to someone like Dr. Q who had memorized more of the Bible than Gil had read—and it wasn't just Q, it was every single person that he met. They were all the coolest people. The pretty, smart, funny, indie bookworm girl was reading books about how to destroy God. The smoker, music snob dude was just into making fun of religious people publicly. That's why Gil and other like-minds ended up just finding it easier to stay undercover. "Turn the other cheek," they would think. Gil did make a friend in one class who must have seen zero signs of Christianese undertones in him. Gil didn't know if he should be proud or ashamed of being incognito, but the long-haired, hipster (who we will call Shroom because of his obsession with psychedelic substances) made a quick chum of Gil nonetheless. Shroom had recently completed and aced a fifty-dollar examination certifying him as an ordained minister in the state of Florida. Shroom didn't know the first thing about running a church, but he had answered thirty questions concerning Christian doctrine with flawless precision, and he could now legally marry John's and Kristy's all over the Belt.

One day, Gil was driving onto campus when he observed a different kind of church signature. Usually, church marquees only served to frustrate Gil and cause him to fantasize about late night vandalism—this one was a genuine attempt to reverse the roll of the things, but probably had failed. This is what it said:

"God is not mad at you."

Had the lecture from Dr. Q not freshly entered Gil's mind, he would have looked at the sign and maybe not gotten frustrated; instead, all he saw was proof of what Q had stated in class. Gil imagined the temple in the Bible that Jesus had wrecked, with a stone tablet suspended high above the courtyard that said, "God is not mad at you." Gil realized that God might in fact be furious with most people. Was the whole love approach a lie just to get people into the church and sway them into a relationship with some God? Perhaps the only way certain people could respond to this love approach was by presenting it to them in the form of a textbook Jonathan Edward's style sulfur pie. Time would tell.

12

ROAD SOUNDS

Gil found himself, over the weekend, sitting at Compass Point in one of those padded, linking chairs that modern churches got together and elected as the new pew. Gray was the new black—chair was the new pew. Wood was so 1999. The Monologue Man had taken the stage and was going on about money and finances and debt and tithing, which was an automatic turnoff for first time visitors—not because of disagreement, but because of most people's standoffishness concerning issues dealing with money in wealthy churches. The Belt played host to a million churches whose pastors had messed up and stolen money in one way or another, so visitors and members wanted to give—they just didn't want to be told to.

The Monologue Man finished speaking—the band played a hype, corporate worship song and the congregation broke for lunch. As Gil joined the mass exodus with the hundreds of Compass Point strangers, he noticed a familiar walk. Wayne was ahead of him, making his way towards a parked motorcycle on the opposite side of the lot. Gil had heard that Wayne recently moved back, but had not seen him yet.

"Wayne!" Gil yelled. Wayne had reached his bike when he turned around to see Gil coming towards him.

"What's up buddy?" Wayne asked.

"Nothing, man. What are you doing here?"

"Ah, I just came to see Bryan. I'm moving again soon."

"Wait, didn't you just move back?"

"Yeah, but you know me. I can't stay in one place too long." Wayne seemed to be sitting on his bike, ready to go.

"Alright, man well good to see you I guess."

"You too, dude. I'll call you or something." With that, he was gone—the loud machine screamed off through the back exit of the parking lot. Gil thought Wayne was pretty badass—like Jesse James.

Gil turned and relocated Nora. He swiftly made his way back and got in on the passenger side of her car. Something had been on her mind all morning—Gil had an idea what it was but kept it to himself.

"That was Wayne," Gil said

"Oh yeah? What's he up to?" Nora asked while looking for her keys in her purse.

"Well he's moving again."

Nora stopped and looked away from the purse for a second.

"Really? Where's he going?"

"Who knows? Why do you seem so distracted and weird?" Gil and Nora had been together for the last few years and Gil could tell when Nora was keeping something. She sucked at secrets. Nora turned to face Gil. The following would be the No. 357 serious relationship talk that would occur inside the cockpit of Nora's blue chick car.

"Remember when I was talking to you about possibly moving up north for college?"

"Yeah. I remember that, Nora," Gil replied with a hint of sarcasm.

"Well, I feel like God has sort of led me to do that now." Gil was back at camp, listening to the Female tell him that God wants her to break up with him. Nora continued.

"I'm moving in a month." Looks like a lonely night at the square dance.

Gil had just changed his life and given up his one and only home—and now the only line that connected him to that home had been severed. He was a man without a country. It's true that when a person moves off to college or something like it, they lose a piece of their home that they will never gain back. Now, days before Gil was to return to summer camp for his last year as a campselor, he was losing it all over again. He spent the next week pouring over the situation. He went for drives a lot. One day he drove past a restaurant whose marquee offered ten percent off meals on Sundays in exchange for church bulletins. Only in the Belt, he thought. Only in the Belt could a restaurant ask to see proof of church attendance for ten percent off a meal and get away with it.

What was it about this place that just made everyone cringe and want to get the hell out of here? Gil had recently heard a story about a seven-year-old boy who stole his parent's car and led the police on a relatively high-speed pursuit through his neighborhood because he didn't want to go to church. Backsliders. Why couldn't Gil be as good at backsliding as everyone else? He suddenly wanted to steal a car and flee the Belt. Five or six years ago, Gil would have viewed the approaching camp experience mountain-top as a welcomed rejuvenation for recent events, but he knew it wasn't going to make a difference now. He would go anyway. He would do his very best to hide a desire to be surprised by God. It was like when you turn a certain age that you deem important, and therefore expect all your friends and family to throw you a surprise party. You pretend like you know it's not happening, but something inside of you really hopes that it does. It doesn't. More people forget than remember.

Three weeks later, Nora had left with nothing more than an "I love you," and an "I'll be praying for you." Gil, having invested all his capacity for companionship into one girl, now stood spinster next to his car, preparing to make one last drive to camp. He would usually plan out music in his head, perfectly themed, to last him the entire two-hour drive through the farm rows, but this time he chose silence. It felt appropriate for the season that he was in. Gil wanted to spend the next couple of hours silently eulogizing his life. The place Gil went to in his head during a silent car ride was a place no human had been. It was like the Holy of Holies. Most people could achieve the Holy of Holies if only they were to give up the noise. Some people just have to have noise. Gil had met several individuals who equated records with gas, in that a car can only move if it has gas inside and a record playing. There are terrific things that can happen in cars with no music.

Gil wondered what the rest of the people from his strange life were doing as he sped his way down country roads passed the greatest of church signs.

God answers knee-mail.

CH__CH—what's missing? U R.

Forbidden fruits create many jams.

Give the devil and inch and he'll be a ruler.

Gil would growl and scream in his car like a caged animal—then his thoughts would return. He would begin to measure the importance of his job at camp, against others his age who were a part of things far different. What was So and So doing at this very moment? Gil felt there was some importance in his returning to camp. He had work to do there, but was it as great a task as that of a mother? So and So had attended camp with Gil not five years ago. Could Gil justify being a counselor for kids when his friends were raising kids? At this very moment, So and So was picking up her son from children's church at First. She had returned on account that no one she knew really went there anymore—the one's she did know didn't really remember or care.

John (of John and Kristy) was joining the Air Force and had just taken his black Pearl drum set out of his garage, shined it up, and put it in the dining room of his bachelor pad. You've all seen these drum sets. You'll be walking in the neighborhood or biking down a quiet street and notice a garage door open. The home belongs to a newlywed couple. Inside the garage is the drum set—tucked between a tower of diapers and unpacked appliances. The Kristy let the John have it, on the condition that it be kept out there.

Kristy (of John and Kristy) had moved back home and was seeing some guy a few years younger than she, a metrosexual looking dude who attended EBJC and played drums for a local indie band. Go figure.

The Everyman was working for men younger than he was; doing work harder than he did when was in the military, for less pay than ever—he didn't complain.

Wayne never left. His bike broke down ten miles out of town and he got his older brother to pick him up.

Nora was finally ignoring every voice but one.

13

Use Less

Camp Oakwood seemed like a lake house that God might come back to visit on occasion. It was almost like Gil could tell whether or not God was going to be joining them during a given summer week. Gil would pull into his spot and check for golden wind chimes over the porch, or a giant "welcome" rug at the front door. Sometimes they were there—sometimes they weren't. The years that Gil didn't immediately see the signs, he and the others would merely assume God was running late. This particular week, Gil's feelings led him to believe that not only were the chimes and rug not there, but the hook that held the chimes was broken, and the front door had been bricked over with some tidy mason work.

It didn't take Gil long to realize that he was alone. Of course he was. Who in their right mind would still be attending camp at his age? Gil settled into his two-person room for one and began wandering the halls, looking for any sign of someone he knew. There were a few kids he had made friends with in previous summers who were several years younger than he was. These were the kids who vowed last year never to stray away from God again—they looked worse than ever. Gil wouldn't have it any other way. He preferred people who were wrecked.

"What's up, Gil? How was your year?" a boy named Cody said from behind.

"Oh, hey man. It was good, dude. How was yours?" Gil answered, turning and putting an arm across Cody's shoulders. Camp Oakwood was the only place in the world one could ask a question like "how was your year?" Everyone there just pretended that camp was the part that mattered. This was real life—the rest was just "year." "How was your year?" was like "how was your drive here?" One year equals one commute to camp.

One of the first things Gil noticed was that the regular week's schedule for Camp Oakwood had been drastically changed from previous years. It seemed as if most of the freedom of the camp experience had been siphoned out and replaced with organized activities designed to increase doctrinal awareness. For the sake of saving arguments, we won't talk about what denomination's doctrine Camp Oakwood subscribed to, but it's safe to say it was one whose more traditional approaches would resurface once a decade and replace the more charismatic ones.

Just after dinner, the students would all be corralled into a sort of great hall setting for an assembly. After counselors were introduced and new kids were sorted into their houses, the camp leader would go over the schedule.

"As you will all notice, our evening worship times have been replaced with Creative Worship. Creative Worship will be when each family group presents a different type of worship. For example, some may do a drama; others may do an interpretive dance, etc. We'll do that for about an hour and then off to snack time and fellowship!" It sounded like a gospel sing to Gil. Given Gil's lack of assigned responsibilities, it seemed as though he would be quite available.

Gil found himself in his room sleeping a lot. Sometimes he would sit and hope that an older, wiser counselor would find him asleep and wake him in a hurried rush of confusion. Hypothetically, it would go something like this:

"Gil! No! Ah-uh! No sleeping right now! You need to get up and go to…" The counselor would become awkward and scour the room for a printed schedule. Gil would stare, rubbing his eyes from beneath the covers.

"Go where?"

"Don't you have a small group in a few minutes?"

"No."

"Well why aren't you teaching your elective class right now?"

"Cause I don't have any talent, and I wasn't assigned one." Gil would say in a sad tone.

"Why are you here then?" the counselor would say, perplexed.

"Not sure…" Gil would reply. Perhaps. Instead, he spent a majority of the week doing nothing. Gil could have honestly seen every single thing as a sign of rejection. He could have spent the whole week feeling sorry for himself and wishing things could change, but instead, he decided to see things as they were. Gil was twenty-something years old with nothing to offer. He viewed himself as an important element to the kids, but so could anyone. Camp Oakwood was going to continue in some form with or without him, so Gil decided to pack up four nights early and leave right then. No, no—just kidding. What kind of upstanding campselor would Gil be if he left his post as night watchman of the boy's dorms?

The one position Gil had been self-appointed to was night watchman. Crazy sorts of things would happen in the boy's dorms at night if there wasn't someone there to regulate the situation. Gil and an older counselor were sitting up late on the last night of camp at a table between the rooms and the lounge area, talking about God's tardiness (or absence) that week as a direct result of control. As it got later, the conversation ran into more bitter words than constructive criticism, so the older counselor decided to go to bed.

"I'm leaving you control of the dorm. You got it?"

"I've got it," Gil replied, as the counselor faded into the darkness in the direction of the staff dorms. Gil liked staying down here. It made him feel more a part of things. Gil, like a good father, went around and turned off the lights and was headed up to his bed when he noticed a light on in another room. Approaching the light, he noticed that all three beds were empty. He sort of panicked a bit.

Gil stood in the quiet hallway and listened carefully. There was nothing at first, and then he noticed whispers coming from a room across and down the hall. Gil quietly crept towards the door. It was pitch black all around him, save for the light of the empty room further back. Something frightened Gil. He felt as if something was behind him. He turned and saw a face at his back.

"Holy—!"

"Shhhhhhh!" It was a familiar face—Cody. Gil turned back and noticed the whispers had stopped.

"Why are you up, Cody?" Gil asked.

"I was going to the bathroom and I saw you walk down here. What's going on?" Cody replied. Gil reached forward and opened the door. The lights were off but Gil could smell the funk of pubescent boys. He turned on the light. They were like six monstrous rats, hiding in the dark. Gil had seen it before—just dudes hanging out together on their last night of camp. There were two on one bed, three on another, and one beneath some covers on the middle bed. Gil stared at them for a minute and laughed.

"What are you guys doing? We have to be up early tomorrow for parents and stuff," Gil reasoned.

"Can we throw chairs, Gil?" said one.

"Gil, please!" said another. Gil heard a voice from over his shoulder.

"Is he naked?" asked Cody, pointing at the boy under the covers. Cody was seriously homophobic. He was one of those guys that just could not joke.

"Yeah," they smiled boyishly.

"Dude, why are you always naked?" Cody asked. The middle boy just smiled. It was true. This was the kid who always found some excuse to be naked when he could be. There was nothing homoerotic going on—just boys being boys in the truest form.

"Listen. I know I did it when I was your age…but throwing chairs just doesn't seem like a good idea tonight," said Gil.

"Well, we're doing it anyway," one said. They all laughed. Gil smiled.

"Think about your brothers, you guys. Everyone is super tired and it's only going to make it worse," Gil replied. Cody stepped in.

"Why don't you guys listen to him? He's trying to be responsible." One of the shirtless boys reached up and put Cody in a headlock. Cody reversed it and had the lost boy begging for mercy within seconds. It was all good fun until the boy, knowing what the result would be, yanked the covers off the naked kid.

"I'm done," Cody said, releasing the headlock and retreating to bed. The boys laughed hysterically at the smiling nudist, lying in his bed like a fetus.

"Look. Do whatever, but go to bed eventually." The boys cheered as Gil closed the door and walked back down the hallway. Gil had not made it far when something touched his ankle in the darkness.

"Hey," whispered a voice at Gil's feet, scaring him half to death. Gil looked down. It was a young camper named Jack. He was lying on a mattress in the hall, inside of a sleeping bag.

"Jack? What are you guys, crazy? Why are you out here?" Gil asked.

"When I got back from snack time tonight, there was someone asleep in my bed, so I found this mattress and put it here," the boy replied.

"Are you sure you're alright out here?"

"Yes. I like it." He was a funny kid. Gil turned and began to walk back down the dark corridor towards his room.

"Gil," whispered the voice. Gil turned and looked back.

"What?"

"I'm glad you're here. I'm glad you're my friend." The boy's face was genuine.

"Thanks, Jack. Try to get some sleep," he whispered back. Gil made his way back towards the light of the empty room. All Gil could think about was what those metal, folding chairs used to sound like, hitting the stone floor, and the deafening silence before collision. He did not want to hear it. Gil exited the dorms and walked through the lounge to a water fountain well out of hearing range of the boys' dubious deed. There he could see through a window, in the light of the moon, those steps where he and Cal had destroyed all that music so many years ago. He took a drink of water and went out to sit. As he settled down onto the top step, a glint from the moon caught his eye in the dirt beneath the wall. When he moved closer, he retrieved a fragment of a CD, worn and weathered from several years of sun and rain. Gil was astonished.

"Lou Bega," Gil laughed, as he pocketed the broken relic. When Gil returned to the table at the foot of the boys dorms, he saw the pile of rusty metal chair silhouettes at the back of the hall where they had slid to a screeching halt. When looking closer, Gil noticed that the chairs were surrounding Jack's makeshift bed. Gil bent down and squinted into the darkness.

"Jack, are you alright?" he whispered loudly. Gil saw a thumbs-up shoot from amidst the chairs.

"I'm good," came the whisper back.

14

FAR AWAY

Several weeks after Camp Oakwood, Gil found himself preparing for his second semester at the big bad university. He hadn't heard from Nora or Wayne all summer, and he was beginning to become used to the idea that he might never see either of them again. They had both escaped the Belt in one way or another. Gil had some kind of unearthly tolerance for the place, however. He didn't hate the idea of living there. Perhaps he escaped the ideological Bible Belt at just the perfect age. Sure, he was still living inside the physical boundaries of the Belt itself, but mentally, he was quite far away.

Gil began to catalog everything that had happened in order to bring him to this point. Gil could remember when he was youngest, thinking that everybody was a Christian: his teacher, his cousin, his pastor. He went to Christian schools, had Christian friends, wore Christian clothes, listened to Christian music, ate Christian food, drank Christian drinks, and smoked Christian crack. The Christian Company had a monopoly stranglehold on the Belt. There were boiled peanut stands on opposite sides of the road; one had a sign that said "Christ Nuts," the other just said "Boiled Peanuts." Guess which one got the business.

Gil became a teenager and found himself growing up in the church youth group. His friends wore cross necklaces and those shirts you've all seen.

Body piercing saved my life.

Someone looking at the shirt might say,
"Yeah! Awesome! Nipple rings! Ah wait…Jesus?! Ah sweet! Where'd you get that?!" Gil's youth group would go to camp, they'd go to retreats, they'd go hang out, and fall in love, and alienate people, and whatever else. Gil would graduate from high school and from youth group and his life would seem to change completely. He'd start attending a new church called Compass Point where everything was cool and catchy and trendy and indie and he'd hear the words: relevant, environment, ministry, element, resource, tool, and art—forty thousand times a year. He'd move on to try and earn his General A.A. at Emerald Breeze Junior College where he'd think he'd met his match in overpowering, professorial intimidation. Someone like Dr. Darmin, notorious for flunking Christians and skilled at shutting

them down, would come along and be the first person in the Belt that Gil ever heard say, "God is not real."

Gil would then split with Nora, split with his friends, and move away to attend a college of higher power. He'd meet people and professors with brains the size of bowling balls, who not only disliked God—they were smarter than Him. The way Gil had envisioned it; every God-hating person that came across his path, merely rejected God because of an instance or occurrence that happened in their lives that caused them to stay far away. If Dr. Q hated God, it was because his dad cheated on his mom. If the pretty, smart, funny, indie bookworm hated God, it was because her best friend had been killed in a car crash. If the smoker, music snob dude hated God, it was because people in church had rejected him his entire life. These were all worthy suspicions, but Gil discovered that most of them were just untrue. Some people just hated God—plain and simple.

That brings Gil to his last hurrah at Camp Oakwood, and the sobering disappointment that although God is omnipresent, sometimes he just doesn't show. Gil could have quite possibly been at the lowest point in his entire life. He didn't feel God. He didn't ask for God. He had forgotten what God looked like. Returning home from camp felt like waking up on the fifth of July and realizing you had missed the fireworks. He had heard the instructions for maintaining a healthy relationship with God time and time again:

1. Read the Bible everyday.
2. Pray constantly.

In essence, it was equivalent to:

1. Read the newspaper at breakfast.
2. Hold conversations with friends.

Granted, the instructions were cake, and Gil knew them back and forth—his house didn't even get the news-paper, and he couldn't discipline his mind enough to hold a conversation with his friends; in fact, many of Gil's friends (especially Nora) would often become irate with Gil's pas-sive interest in the imperative conversational element of call and response.

Gil was terrible at small talk. This handicap also made it virtually impossible to speak to Christians. He had no problem talking to non-Christians—he didn't have to re-ally keep the dialogue aimed in any particular direction, just talk. A lot of times, Gil viewed himself the same way Shroom viewed him. Shroom saw Gil as the normal person he was. Although their conversations sometimes went to lower places than others, they were conversations nonethe-less that Gil didn't feel had to live up to anything special. Gil would sometimes catch Shroom repeating something Gil had said to him in an earlier conversation, but instead of reciting it verbatim, he would insert some harsher phras-ing that Gil never really implied. Was this just Shroom adding his own twist to the story, or did he really see Gil carelessly throwing around various forms of off-color vo-cab? Was there even a difference between Gil and Shroom?

Gil often wondered had he not grown up in the Belt, would he still think and feel the way he did now? Had Gil been beaten as a child, raised by alcoholics, and never taken to church—would he not want to have anything to do with God? Or put another way; had Gil been pampered as a child, raised by aristocrats, and taken to piano practice every Wednesday—would he try his very hardest to disprove God with all the intellectual and mechanical willpower he could muster? He was almost certain that had his life not been completely branded by the words of his parents, pastors, teachers, and friends—he would have been irrevocably different. Realizing this, Gil wanted to renovate his mind, and withdraw all the parts of his thinking that had been passively inserted into his head, and start all over.

Gil knew three things: The first was that in the Belt, there was a deity called God (with a big G). This God, according to Christian tradition, was the Father of a man who came to Earth and was tried as a heretic and sentenced to execution. His execution was subsequently the payment for all sin committed by all humans before, during, and after his death. After being dead for three days, God's son resurrected, and met several witnesses to whom he gave brief instructions to continue what he started in spreading his story. Since then, the religion named for Jesus Christ has become the single most influential and widely spread religion in the history of man. Believing in this story, and identifying with the claim that this God's son is the means by which one may escape eternal death and gain eternal life, will in fact grant one said eternal life. These were the facts; the core root system of Christianity presented to Gil. Beyond Gil's feeble understanding of various personal, spiritual encounters, he reasoned from a mental approach that there were several very mechanical pieces of information that appealed cognitively to intellectual approaches and therefore assisted Gil in reasoning mentally that Jesus was who he said he was, and those tidbits were nothing he learned in Sunday school.

The second thing Gil knew was that fellowship was an elemental part of growth. Gil had been made all of his life to go to church. The question remains, had Gil never been forced, would he have gone anyway? When viewing it from a Biblical point, Gil saw that Jesus (while on Earth) traveled with followers called disciples. Gil didn't have any disciples, but he knew that some of the darker, more undesirable moments of his life had been spent while in solitude. He knew that humans were meant to congregate and grow. When Gil was younger, he lived in a neighborhood in the middle of the woods. He lived in a neighborwood. This neighborwood was situated along a vast stretch of two-lane highway leading to Indian River. It always fascinated Gil how he could be so far away from civilization, but there were always people huddled together. He would often view each individual house as a person or a family, when upon stepping back to observe the picture; they appeared to be a group of people, protected.

This law of nature was enough to convince Gil of the need for people to be with people and share life together. The Bible Belt translation of this togetherness was the church. Gil believed that church fellowship was an important factor in the growth of a Christian, but he didn't really think that what most Belter churches were offering people was enough. Gil's mindset shifted from the mentality that it is right to attend the church of father and mother and make it the church of Gil. It was hard for Gil to see how there could be a universal set of ideals that could be adopted by all denominations and factions of the Christian faith. He had heard about some churches splitting because of disagreements over which side of a sanctuary the Christian flag should be placed in reference to the American flag. He had heard about some churches splitting because of disagreements over which translation of the Bible is truly God-breathed. He had even heard about some churches splitting over the decision to replace old lawn marquees with newer, digital ones with the ability to display seven genius quips a week. Gil felt the chances were slim to none that when God's man-son left his friends with instructions on building his church, he intended on their being thirty-four thousand foundations with additional ones forming everyday. He did, however, find it obvious that certain churches work better for certain people.

The third and final thing that Gil knew was that the definition of the word "Christian" had changed and was changing everyday. There was something about the word that had just become more of a brand than a way to be. There was Christian this and Christian that—Gil wondered if he could be rid of the name without being rid of its pertinence. Gil didn't know what Christian was, but he thought he had a fair grasp on what it wasn't. While growing up, being a Christian meant that you walk through the motions and cast all the judgments and appease all the elders and teachers and deacons and whoever. These were all the things that rudimentary teachings had told him. When changing his format and subscribing to the more modern Christian agenda, he came across some people who lived on the opposite side of the fence. Most of these people had grown up attending churches like First or St. Luke's and unfortunately, they had tasted a bitter piece of legalism. When they decided to find other churches, they found a "freedom" they had never experienced or abused before.

Gil never questioned whether it was wrong to drink—wrong to smoke, until now. When Gil was younger, his internal bells would ring when he witnessed someone doing either. Long before he went to Compass, Gil became an advocate for the whole "Jesus drank, 'do not be drunk with wine,' everything in moderation," argument. Rather than remaining under that banner, Gil wondered why he and others were still talking about drinking being a sin after two thousand years. Better yet, he wondered why he and others participated in many extra-ecclesiastical activities with zero accountability. Gil figured it had something to do with circumcision. He was taught during some long-lost Bible lesson, that certain people would designate themselves as Godly, by undergoing circumcision. Babies are circumcised today for health reasons and whatnot, but then—it was merely an act of exclusivity. Gil hoped this didn't mean that every male claiming to be a Christian should go out and snip off his foreskin, but he could see the parallel, he supposed. Perhaps the word "Christian" implied something different.

Those were the three things that Gil knew. He would start with just three. A total overhaul of all theological upbringing would prove to be a daunting task; after all, he was quite far away.

15

Rock Bottom

Welcome to Rock Bottom! This is the mental place where people end up just before Hell. Here at Rock Bottom, we allow people to have one final chance to return to the surface and accept the conditions of surrender to Almighty God. Will you yield in time?

"Rock Bottom" is a term used by many Belters when referring to that stint of time wherein a given individual will hit an all-time low. It's not a literal place but it is all-too-often the idealistic oasis that certain people deem as the last stop before losing your salvation and being plunged into the abyss. Many times, the term will be used in conjunction with a given individual coming to a realization of their behaviors and state of existence, and then turning from their ways in order to rejoin the "righteous life."

Someone might say, "After my mom died, I lost my job, my car, my house, my friends, and found myself doing lines of coke off a toilet seat —it was then that I realized I had hit rock bottom." Gil could remember how the term was thrown around when he was younger. Someone would stand up at church or Bible study during a sharing time and would tell about their close call with death. The person would have been out living a frivolous life (whatever that may mean) and they would tell about how they had reject-ed God and didn't need him and whatnot. They would go into further detail about getting drunk one night and driv-ing off an interstate entrance ramp and surviving. That was their moment of rock bottom. They immediately realized that God was saying something to them and they listened.

If there was such a place as Rock Bottom, Gil wasn't sure he had made it yet. Wayne had been there before; in fact, he had been there on numerous occasions. Wayne had a summerhouse in Rock Bottom. The difference for him was that he never would fully resurface. Wayne kind of chilled close to the void that led there.

The Everyman had also frequented Rock Bottom during certain parts of his life. His first visit was in the '60s during Vietnam. His mother had been dead for years and the man with the wiry beard had finally followed her. The Everyman was ripe with hatred for the sailor, and he quaked in anger at the fact that he had never gotten to confront him. In a rage, The Everyman gladly accept-ed his selection into the fatigues and funneled his disdain through a gas powered Browning M2HB .50cal air-cooled machine gun. He would only realize years and years later that he had been there, then. Other visits to Rock Bottom included: divorce, joining old crowds, and pretty much all of the 70's. When referring to individuals whose lives lack the color of Wayne and the Everyman—the terms have to change. In order for one to understand the type of Rock Bottom that Nora could have possibly encountered, it requires a different set of conditions. Nora's Rock Bottom most likely occurred just before she and Gil called it quits and she headed north in an attempt to answer some call that had been ringing since birth. This difference in low points was what caused Gil to question the idea that there is one universal Rock Bottom for everyone.

It even caused Gil to question whether the entire idea of a place like Rock Bottom is just something invented by Christians in the Bible Belt in order to keep people from killing themselves when they got there.

Gil envisioned Rock Bottom as a broken machine. It was like when people get tattoos or try whiskey or watch a porno—the harder the hit, the easier it is to go there next time. So in essence, Rock Bottom was a place where once reached, one could return on command, and in actuality, stand it a bit more each time. People say, "oh I don't ever want to go back there again," but when it's as close as you can get to attaining whatever it was you were aiming for anyway, why not go back?

Gil was in the middle of his fall term at school, driving home one weekend to see his brothers, Grey, and mom when he received a voicemail on his cell phone. It was Nora. Gil hadn't heard from her in over a year except for a "hope all is well" text here and there. She was in town visiting her parents and she wanted to meet for lunch. She said she'd be at the bulletin place tomorrow at one o' clock. She understood if he didn't want to come, so she left it open-ended. Of course Gil would go. It was just a matter of getting her to shut up on the voicemail so he could call her back.

An hour or so later, Gil was sitting at the dining room table in his house with his mom, Grey, and his brothers.

"Oh, I know what we should all do—tomorrow night; First is having that fall festival!" exclaimed Gil's mom. The men slanted their heads and gaped at her, but they would go as a favor to mom. Gil's weekend was slowly being planned for him.

Gil found a quiet moment to retreat to his room for the night to prepare himself to meet Nora the next day for lunch.

The next morning, Gil woke up on purpose. He ate a bowl of cereal and read the front couple pages of the newspaper. It was only after Gil had left the house and driven halfway to meet Nora that afternoon that he remembered his house didn't even get the newspaper. What the hell was going on? Traffic seemed to be really backed up for some reason, which wasn't too typical at this time of day. Gil assumed Malcolm was driving his power-chair in the carpool lane again. Then he saw it. Justice Faith Tabernacle (a particularly straight-laced, strict-walking group of bike-riding, holy-rollers) had taxed the intersection. They were doing the usual—berating drivers with bullhorns, sticking their heads inside car windows, and shooting rounds of scripture off with their Bible-guns. Gil had come to a stop at a red light.

"Wah wah wah wah wawawawah wa!" they all said. Gil rolled down his window a bit so he could hear beyond the mumbles. It sounded like something from a Blake poem:

"Repent Backsliders! 'Mark well my words, they are for your eternal salvation!'"

"You are on a downward spiral to Hell, sir! Turn or burn!" Gil rolled the window back up and noticed the light ahead had turned green and it was now his turn to attempt to pass them. Gil gunned it, but before he knew it, the light had turned red again. He was in trouble. It was honestly a matter of seconds before they descended on his car like a flock of buzzards on the flesh of carrion.

"You in there! You are going to Hell!" came the call from one side.

"Roll down your window and hear the good news!" from the other. Gil figured he better man-up. He didn't have anything better to do with his next sixty seconds. He rolled down the window. The nicely dressed boy—black pants, white button shirt, and black tie—brandished the bullhorn like a weapon and put it right inside Gil's window.

"You are headed straight for the lake of fire!" Gil felt like his ears were bleeding, and then suddenly his head went silent. There was a faint hum of someone yelling, and his mind drifted to a far away memory of being in an almost identical situation with Wayne. Gil and Wayne were stopped at the very same intersection with the very same group of people some odd years ago. Wayne rolled down the passenger-side window and signaled for one of the shouters to come over. Wayne waited for the perfect moment. As the bullhorn entered the car, he grabbed the device at its base and yanked it from the shouter's grasp. Just then, the light turned green, Wayne rolled the window up, and Gil peeled away. It was legendary.

Perhaps Dr. Q's prediction had come true and the sulfur pie approach really had come full circle. Maybe love had lost its potency and the effective approach for reaching people had become bullhorning them until their ears bled—but no one was listening; not then, not now. People went on about their lives—taking their kids to baseball practice, driving to lunch, getting their oil changed, calling their families, listening to music, and hearing their road sounds. Back in the present, Gil awoke from his daydream to a shout from the bullhorn.

"Sir...the light's green." Gil looked forward and noticed there were no cars in front of him. He hit the gas and within minutes, was pulling into the restaurant to meet Nora.

Gil entered the restaurant, bypassed the counter and went straight over to Nora. She stood up from the booth and smiled. She was wearing jeans, black slip-ons, a black tank top, and a black headband.

"What's up, Ozzy?" Gil said. Nora did one of those cute girl smiles, trying to seem playfully offended.

"Nothing. How are you doing?" she replied. They sat down on opposite sides.

"I'm doing well. How are you doing? What've you been up to?" Gil asked.

"Ah, everything's just been going awesome lately. I'm interning at this place up there where they do social work for kids that are pulled out of these really dangerous situations. It's really intense. What about you? What have you been doing? How's school?"

"Yeah, school's going really well, just trying to finish everything up next semester. You know, I'm not really doing anything that important like saving kids' lives or anything. I went to Oakwood again this summer."

"Well that's important, Gil. That place wouldn't be what it is to those kids without you there."

"Ah, I have a feeling it would."

"Well," Nora reasoned. The table went silent for a few seconds and Gil tried desperately to build up enough confidence to ask Nora the burning question. She interjected.

"Oh! Katy's here, by the way. She's in the bathroom." Just then, Katy, a youthy friend of both Nora and Gil's, came walking around the corner. Gil was finished.

"Katyyyyyyyy…" he slurred with a fake smile as he stood to hug the girl who was infamous for always being at the wrong place at the wrong time.

"Hey, Gil. Good to see you," she said. Katy was nice, just wrong. She sat down on Nora's side and soon had a huge salad in front of her. The three did their best to keep the conversation afloat. Gil and Nora made occasional eye contact during Katy's attempt to explain the last year in the Belt through a mouthful of salad.

An hour went by. The three of them got up and made their way outside. Gil had parked next to Nora's blue chick car.

"I'll let you guys talk. Nora, can I have your keys?" Katy said. Nora handed her the keys and Katy disappeared into the car.

"Well, it was good to see you," Nora said.

"Yeah, you too," Gil replied as he gave her a hug. Gil was at the point now where he realized the meeting was never intended to reunite the two of them.

"I'm glad to hear that everything is working out like you hoped," said Gil.

"Well, most of it is," Nora replied.

"Alright, well I'll see you later."

"Bye, Gil." They had one last hug and turned to their cars. Gil took the long way home to avoid the Tabernacle. Nora hit the intersection just as the boys were at their very best.

That night, Gil found himself riding with his brothers to the First United Methodist Fall Festival. He was fourteen again—or he felt like it. The Christian alternative to Halloween was nothing like he remembered it. When Gil was younger, First's fall festival was a sight to behold. The sheer number of people was what always amazed him. They called it 'Hallelujah Night,' because it sounded sort of close to Halloween. The reason Gil liked it so much back then was because of the loads of candy available. There wasn't a trick-or-treat'er in town that could gather more candy than Gil after spending his night traversing mazes themed after the sewers of Egypt, or playing "pin the tail on Jesus' donkey." The fall festival of the twenty-first century was quite different. There were maybe—maybe thirty people there. There were a few booths scattered around with games like: toss-a-sack, jump-a-rope, throw-a-ball, and the 'stick your hand in the bucket of candy and get what you want' game.

"They should call this 'Fail-festival," said Gil's middle brother.

"Why don't we go over and stick our heads in that bucket of sweat," said the oldest—referring to the 'bob-an-apple' booth. Gil laughed as Grey and mom joined the group.

"Looks like you brought the whole mess of 'em tonight Grey!" It was him—the Everyman. He was high on cotton candy and had Tootsie-Roll stuck in his teeth. Like a charm, the people came running.

"Hey boys. How's work? How's Calvary Praise? How's the belly of the whale?" By Calvary Praise, they meant Compass Point, but didn't care enough to get it right.

"Hey. Fine. Awesome. Cozy." Gil wandered off by himself in hopes that he might get his hands on some actual food, when from behind came a call,

"Gil!" He turned to see So and So approaching with what must have been her son.

"Hey! How's it going?" Gil hugged her and greeted the boy.

"What's up bud?"

"Nothin'," came the reply.

"This is Mr. Gil, can you say hi?" So and So said to the boy.

"Hey," he said. They laughed a bit like awkward people do. So and So bent down to her son's level.

"Hey, why don't you go over there and try out the "hammer-a-nail" booth, alright?" The boy ran off to wreak some havoc on the sheet-wood full of rusty metal spikes.

"So everything's going well I suppose?" Gil asked.

"Yeah, really great. We've had our ups and downs but who hasn't? After you hit Rock Bottom there's really nothing that seems that bad." There was that term again. Where was this place and why had everyone been there?

"Yeah, I guess so," replied Gil. They talked a bit more. So and So told Gil about school and church and family— the regular Belter stuff, and then they parted ways. Gil did catch a glimpse of Kristy at the "paint-a-face" booth, but they didn't speak.

The next morning was Sunday. Gil thought he'd head over to Calvary Praise and hear what the Monologue Man had to say. Gil counted his way through the message. The Monologue Man hit on every one of the seven words. Bingo. The band played a song and then the lasers dimmed out like on "Who Wants to be a Millionaire?" The Monologue Man began a closing prayer. As he spoke, Gil lifted his head and looked across the worship center at his friend Nora. Her head was lowered and her hair was covering her face. Gil began to wonder what things had come out of his life. What had he accomplished as a twenty-something with nothing to offer? He thought about all the things that had shaped he and Nora into who they were. The Bible Belt had been more than a place to the two of them. It had been less than a place to a lot of others. Gil's life in the Belt was one that had shifted weight over and over. One phase of his life had him believing in a God that was infinitely different from the one he believed in now. Both Gods were ultimately the same, housed within the same shell, but they were subjectively unique in all respects. He understood that there was a place that many people go just before something makes them better. Gil understood that he may never need to go to that place, but as blatantly as some people ask for it, and as confused as that made Gil, he understood that for some, Rock Bottom is more than just a cliché. For some, it's hope.

Gil awoke the next morning with a splitting headache. He stumbled his way out of his room and across the kitchen to get some aspirin when he heard a knock at the door. He ran over to the microwave to fix his hair. What if it was Nora coming around to say goodbye? He did a quick poof-n-swoop on his morning mullet and answered the door. Gil didn't know whose Rock Bottom this was, but it could have very well been his own. Wayne stood before him in all the glory of the Justice Faith Tabernacle black and white attire. Gil wanted it to be a joke—but it wasn't.

There were two other Tabernacle boys standing behind him on either side with Bibles and bullhorns in-hand.

"Wayne?" Gil said in utter disbelief.

"Gil, I'm so glad we caught you at home. Are you aware that you are on a downward spiral to Hell?"

16

MEGABLOG

The foot locker in the shed was where his father kept the less-than-savory things. And he had kept them a long time. He knew so because of their hair—the women in the magazines. Perms and bangs, teased to the high heavens. They were from an age when ladies seemed older; more motherly. Nothing matched the matriarchs of today (not even their endowment). He paused for a moment to thumb through the images, and then pushed them aside. After all, they weren't what he'd come for. His true spoils lay beneath several more layers of bones, booze and buried treasure. The thing that would finally make him visible.

***

Gil sat at his desk, mentally retracing his steps. He was dumbfounded at how things had escalated so quickly. In the last five years, he'd inadvertently made a career of picking fights with middle-aged moms on social media. He must have been crazed to travel back down that digital trail of tears to the land from where he and the rest of his tribe had been banished. After all, the weapons of the White Woman were far superior. Whether it was a quip about public breastfeeding or some sarcasm of how useful college was (the things Gen-X moms rage about), he was always mitigating some defensive rant that would never in a million years take place at church or in the grocery aisle. This time in particular, Gil had posted about a moral issue. The mistake being that he'd chosen to base his argument on a book written by dead Jewish guys instead of on a clever meme from a popular atheist page. One friend, several comments back, had even tried to resolve the tension, but was sorely unsuccessful.

Gil: I didn't say that.

Dan: Let's all be friends :P

Stella Graves-Levinworth: You implide it.

Stella Graves-Levinworth: implied*

These days, Gil was the Minister of Blogs at Compass Point.

Yes. That's right. Mega churches love their obscure titles. He wasn't quite sure what the object of the position was—maybe to thin out the herd with unpopular theology. According to that definition, he was doing a standup job.

"I'm just gonna delete it," Gil said, staring at his Mac. He had hoped to garner the attention and support of his fellow coworkers, but no one cared. "And maybe shoot myself. Yeah, that."

"Dude!" A coworker next to him exclaimed somewhat sarcastically. "Not cool! Not today!" The communal office space was otherwise quiet, except for the faint sound of someone strumming the chords to a corporate worship tune on a muted Tele in the next room.

"Anyone else home?" Gil playfully ignored. The same guy in the Ikea-chic work stall next to him removed his headphones in mock impatience and obliged.

"What's the problem?" His name was Conroy, and his first name was a last name. Gil imagined that Conroy had asked people to call him that in order to set him apart from other mega church media guys (or to make himself exactly the same). As if his ape-ish beard and PBR belly didn't accomplish that already. Seriously, he looked ready to eat the face off a bear.

"Is it hard to breathe with your shirt buttoned all the way up to the neck like that?" Gil asked, gesturing.

"You're a jerk," Conroy said quick and quiet as he reinserted his earbuds.

"Anybody check out the numbers from this weekend?" another coworker said from across the room. "Attendance was off the hook! Worship was sick! Just another week in the kingdom, baby!"

"What?" Gil said under his breath.

"You guys know Stella Graves?" Gil's supervisor asked.

"Country singer," someone said.

"No," his supervisor replied. "She's this rad volunteer who serves on the Pinpoint Team. She's having a benefit art show downtown Saturday for the 20th anniversary."

Stella Graves (hyphen) Levinworth was coincidentally the same Urban Outfitters mom with six beautiful, Arian offspring who was currently berating Gil one punctuation-free comment at a time. He kept quiet, clicking the delete button on the thread.

"Dope..."

***

There were more than a handful of establishments in Indian River where one might acquire a suitable sidearm on short notice. Short enough to satiate more demanding impulses; those brought on by sudden fits of anger or rage-induced revenge- dealing. He needed it for neither. The boy was first and foremost, calm. There was no rage about it. No blood boiling in his veins. There was only the moment. He was internal, and far too young to get his hands on anything by way of traditional channels (even on the edge of town), so it didn't matter anyway. The metal was cold against his forearm, broken only by the wooden stocks and leather strap. He traced the serial number with his finger and looked at his watch. It was Sunday.

***

"Shellfish. That's all I'm saying." Gil's wife was building a case. "I love me some crab legs."

"Please don't ever say that again," Gil said. "And that's a tired argument. I'm tired of people making claims based on their SparkNotes knowledge of something as dense as the Bible."

"It's just not a very likable mindset."

"Who said we were supposed to be likable?!" Gil bellowed.

"You wanna watch Lost?" she asked.

"Yep." It was easier for Gil these days to ignore the state of things than to acknowledge the fact that it felt very much like the church had become just another toppling paradigm. He missed the Megabelt at its pinnacle! At least then you weren't surprised by people (or they had sense enough to shut up). This was the age of Moralism as a religion. The age of the Mod Church.

The Mod Church methods worked. People joined the cause, and lives turned corners, but Gil often wondered if the plan was creating north and south poles between the "churched" and the "unchurched" like there had been before. Mod Church was the new tradition; something that was proven to work. But The Great Awakening wasn't great because it was proven, it was great because it was bold and fleeting. By today's standards it might have seemed incredibly boring to sit through, especially after so many years. Gil knew tons of people from his parents' generation who were wishin' and hopin' and thinkin' and prayin' for another one of these "revivals" to come and sweep them off their feet, but they'd missed it entirely. The Mod Church had been the revival, in all its protein-baked beauty. Gil had this theory that all Mod Churches, Christianese conferences and youth groups got their names from protein supplements.

Core. Rip'd. Fuse. Shred. Edge. Break.

Even Gil's jokes had lost their luster in light of the Belt crumbling. The Mod Church had already been satirizing itself on YouTube for half a decade. Gil figured the expiration date on anything edgy was when people grew so familiar with it that it became funny. No one makes fun of baseball because of how it's played, the damage is done when you realize there are 162 games in a single season. You do anything the same way for too long and it always sucks.

***

No one noticed his bag that morning, even with the barrel sticking straight out of the zipper as he walked in the church and arrived at his classroom. It wasn't that unusual, really. He wasn't often paid attention to. Only one youngster with donut glaze crusted lips had inquired about it mockingly.

"Show and tell," he replied. It would only be a matter of time before his Sunday school classmates all remembered it was his turn to share, so he knew he couldn't keep it hidden for long. He could feel the anticipation building inside. Finally, they would see him. Finally, they would know.

***

Gil figured he might be cast overboard soon enough for rocking the boat too hard. He didn't own one of those convenient cardboard file boxes to pack his desk flair into at a moment's notice. He thought about investing in one soon. It was lunch time now, and Gil was starving. Not Somalian kid starving, but hungry enough for Taco Bell to sound right.

"Could I get a beef and potato burrito, grilled, with nacho cheese and no sour cream. Like, none at all."

"Sure thing, man," said the pubescent man-child behind the counter. "So how's it going?"

Gil glanced behind him and back. "...good?" he asked. The question had just caught him off guard. He wasn't used to being buddied up by Taco Bell guys.

"You work at Compass, right? I'm the new H.R. intern."

"Yes! Oh, sorry!," Gil apologized. "I didn't recognize you." He still didn't. It was a regular occurrence to be spotted by churchies he couldn't place.

"No worries, man. This is my paying gig. Hey, you gonna be at REFUEL tonight?" REFUEL was the once-a-month, mid-week spiritual pep rally that all Mod Churches offered their members.

"Um, maybe. Probably. I don't know."

"Going to FREEDOM720 this year?"

"What?"

"WAVE? EPICENTER? What Life Group are you in?"

"Oh, well my wife and I are actually taking the semester off because—"

"—Don't do life alone, brother! Haha, Yes!" He came in for a bro grab over the counter.

"Oh, ok—" Gil obliged awkwardly. "—Here's your food, man."

"Thanks..."

He felt like he'd been assaulted. The burrito was almost all sour cream.

After lunch, Gil found himself ignoring work and stalking Stella Graves-Levinworth on Facebook. She and her family had apparently already resolved to leave Compass and attend a newer, hotter, bustier church downtown.

Stella Graves-Levinworth: It is my pleasure to announce that Robert and I have decided to join Creek Bed Baptist! We went to our first family grope last night and have never felt so welcomed by a community of people. We feel very confirmed and so excited for our first Sunday! Ya'll come check us out!!!!1

Stella Graves-Levinworth: group*

Gil had caught the tale of this resurgence in traditional denominations to recapture what they'd lost in the wake of the Mod Church boom. And they were doing a damn good job. It was the same thing as Sunbeam combating local farmer's markets with a collection of artisan breads or Nike creating a line of canvas shoes made by Kenyan cobblers. They were great products; easy to consume and far superior in longevity, just late to the game.

For the first time in five years, Gil thought about the church where he grew up. His parents didn't talk about First very much, but he was sure they too must have been adopting some of these latent practices. After all, the trail had already been blazed. It would have just been wasteful for the big denoms with the big money to not come along and pave it all up. He kept reading.

***

It was over before it started. The bullet from the teacher's gun had travelled straight through the boy's brain as soon as he'd lifted the rusted relic into view. It was almost a reflex, though she kept the weapon in her purse for such once- per-lifetime occasions. She was a public school teacher during the week, after all, and it was the '90s. A sense of pride surged through her at first, as she held the pistol extended before her with both hands. She was a hero. Then a haunting realization crept over her amidst the cries of the children and the noise of church patrons storming the room in slow motion. It was the recollection of what she'd requested of the boy the Sunday before: "Make sure it's something really special!"

***

Rebecca Hooper: Sad you guys are leaving Compass :(Mind if I ask why? DM me?

Stella Graves-Levinworth: It's not a secret. We just learned the church has some saddening viewpoints.

Rebecca Hooper: What happened?

Stella Graves-Levinworth: They posted a very pro-life blog, and I shared my differing views. One thing led to another and the topic shited to the 20th anniversary...

Stella Graves-Levinworth: Shifted*

Stella Graves-Levinworth: The only reason the event even took place was because Christians discouraged that woman from terminating her pregnancy. I mean, look how that little boy grew up. It was destiny.

Rebecca Hooper: Wow, I never thought of that!

Stella Graves-Levinworth: Tragedy.

Gil's index finger was on the button. He wanted so badly to say something smart. Something for the books. It was the 20th anniversary of a disaster that was later proven to be a grave misunderstanding. Gil's comment was nothing but a reiteration of that fact, and he knew deep down it would accomplish nothing. In the end, it was all about control, the same as with everything else, and he could stand to give it up. The Belt was at war with itself; like underwear brothers, fighting over the remote, and the only choices are the Weather Channel or Matlock. Gil held the delete button until every last letter was erased from memory. Something told him he'd made the right choice.

A smiling face then peeked around the corner of his stall.

It was the nameless man-child intern from the church's H.R. department and Taco Bell.

"Gil, You're fired."

GLOSSARY OF BELTER TERMS

A

Abstinence – An ancient practice once observed by monks and nuns; now adopted by Christians and others, dealing with saving the act of sexual intercourse for marriage or never.

Altar – A place of prayer positioned at the front of a church where everyone goes but no one wants to be.

Anti-Patriotic – Having to do with one's refusal to follow conditions of normality.

Art – Anything—apparently

Authority Figure – A parent or adult on staff (or who believes they're on staff) at a church.

B

Backslider – Anyone not attending church.

Belter – Someone who lives or works in the Bible Belt.

Big G Syndrome – The belief that God will strike one dead for spelling His name with a lower-case letter.

Bla bla – Belter talk.

Bowling Alley – A breeding ground for young youth group love.

C

Camp – Mecca for Belters.

Chick Car – Any car that a straight man would feel uncomfortable driving.

Christian – Anything made clean by the mention of God or Jesus.

Christianese – An ancient language spoken by Belters.

Christian Comedian – Someone who tells jokes that are only funny because the humor bar has been lowered significantly while at camp or on retreats.

Church League Softball Game – Christian sports.

Church Sign (Marquee) – personal billboards where pastors and Christian business owners may freely display their own opinions and thoughts – even if no one wants to hear them.

Courting – A ritual wherein two strangers spend a set amount of time getting to know each other over coffee with their parents before getting married.

Covered Dish – An array of ice-cold food.

D

E

Element – A thing.

Environment – A place.

Evangelist – A preacher from out of town (similar to greener grass.)

F

Fellowship – Time spent at church, away from the sanctuary.

Foosball – An ancient game where boys try to score goals with wooden soccer players while attempting to avoid being jabbed in the testicles by metal rods.

G

Generation Y – Offspring of Generation X

God – The Christian deity.

god – Any pagan deity.

God Experience – Any strand of time when one feels a particular closeness to God mixed with happiness to be away from home and around different people.

Go-Kart Track – The place where all Belter youth groups are trying to get.

Good Samaritan – Someone who feels a temporary urge to share a God overload with those who don't need or want it.

Gospel Sing – A Southern talent show.

Green Funk of the Belt – The visual smell that accompanies Belters everywhere they go.

H

Holy Landmark – Places where Belter youth groups go.

Holy of Holies – A place achieved in an automobile when thought replaces music.

Homegrown – Belter for "lame."

Home School – A means of education whose curriculum is a set of field trips.

I

Ice Cream Social – The reward for making it through a gospel sing.

Intra-Group Camp Relationship – Relationships that last 1-2 days while on youth trips.

J

Junior College – 13th and 14th grade.

K

L

Liberal Nugget – A surprise piece of unexpected adversity in the Belt.

M

Male A – Good guy; you.

Male B – Bad guy; him.

Marital Sex – The Holy Grail for Belter boys (and some girls).

Mega Church – The largest gathering of strangers in the world.

Molestache – Any facial hair native to a pedophile's face.

Mountaintop – The highest possible spiritual plateau for Christians.

N

Non-Baptist – Anyone eating lunch after 11:30 A.M.

Non-Charismatic Christian – Anything outside of a Christian bookstore.

O

Off-Month – Boring times in a youth group.

P

Ping Pong – An arena for Belter's to showcase useless athletic coordination. A green table with two wooden paddles and a lost ball.

Porn-esque – 1% or less of actual sex.

Post-Camp Question – "Why can't I maintain that feeling after camp is over?"

Potluck – See "Covered Dish."

Pregnancy Scare – Wondering if conception can be accomplished remotely.

Q

Quadruple By-Pass Church Transplant – The act of leaving one church and joining another.

R

Rally – An event intended to stir up emotions; emotions that don't last longer 12 minutes.

Red Line – The mental line that exists between any two successive sexual advances.

Relevant – Something applicable today.

Repentance – A strong apology for sin.

Resource – Any tangible extension of church doctrine.

Revival – An extended mountaintop experience.

Rockslide – A southern roller coaster.

S

Satanic – Anything having to do with a witch.

School/Church Hybrid – Christian School

Season – A particular time in life.

Secular – Anything not mentioning God or Jesus.

Seeker-Friendly – An environment that attracts people.

Self-Fulfilling Prophecy – A word that is only made true by one's self.

Skating Rink – A place where a fast-forward relationship is birthed, experienced, and ended all in a matter of one night.

Small Group – Sunday school in a living room.

Spiritual Awakening – A moment of heightened spiritual interest.

Square Dance – A southern prom.

Stadium Whisper – A whisper that can be heard by thousands of people—therefore making zero sense and defeating its purpose.

Stagnant – Any period of time in-between moments of spiritual awakening.

Student Leader – twenty-first century term for a "youth leader."

Stuff – Any sort of sexual act between kissing and intercourse.

Sulfur Pie – A message intended to save people by scaring them into salvation.

Sunday School – A Small Group that takes place in a church.

T

Tent Revival – Identical to a circus except typically without animals.

Testimony – An interesting or compelling story to share with a group of strangers.

The Back Pews – An observation area of a church.

The Female – A girl who is only attractive in church or church settings.

The Vault – An area where dads keep forgotten or unused gifts, (i.e. closets or dressers).

Tool – See "Resource."

True Love Waits – An event meant to keep teenagers from having sex.

Twenty-Something - Someone in their twenties without so much as a name.

U

V

W

Winter Months – The three months of the year that the Belt gets cold.

Worship Center – A mega church's sanctuary.

X

Y

Youth Band – Where Belter talent is accidentally first stumbled upon.

Youth Group – See chapter entitled "Youth Group."

Youthy – Someone in or having to do with a youth group.

Z

Nick May is the twenty-something native Floridian author behind the oil-slicked satirical thriller MINUTEMEN and the fanatical occult mystery MOLECRICKET. He lives along the Gulf Coast with his wife Kayla and their dog Brother. Find Nick online at heynickmay.com, facebook.com/ heynickmay or follow him on Twitter and Instagram @heynickmay.

Different?

Off the beaten track?

Positively Weird?

But it's solid art?

Look for it!
Publish it!
at
Eucatastrophe Press
eucatastrophepress.com

More fiction from
Energion Publications Imprints

Enzar Empire Press

Tales from Jevlir: Oddballs	Henry E. Neufeld	$9.99
Day of the Dragon	Joseph G. Whelan	$24.99

enzarempire.com

Eucatastrophe Press

Megabelt (2nd Edition)	Nick May	$12.99
Minutemen (2nd Edition)	Nick May	$12.99
The Fringe (forthcoming in 2015)	Renee Crosby	$9.99

eucatastrophepress.com

Energion Publications

Allegheny Hideaway	Kimberly Gordon	$16.99
Covenant	Daniel Martin	$17.99
Please Love Me	Kimberly Gordon	$14.99
Prayer Trilogy	Kimberly Gordon	$9.99
The Traveler's Advance	Heath Taws	$14.99
Stories of the Way	Henry E. Neufeld	$9.99

energion.com

Generous Quantity Discounts Available
Dealer Inquiries Welcome
Energion Publications — P.O. Box 841
Gonzalez, FL 32560
Website: energion.com
Phone: (850) 525-3916

www.ingramcontent.com/pod-product-compliance
Lightning Source LLC
Chambersburg PA
CBHW020915180626
46816CB00007BA/2407